For an instant ti

She was aware only of the beating of her heart and of him.

Rachel imagined that this was what a lover's touch must feel like. Tender. Soft. Gentle.

This man, she realized, was doubly dangerous.

Not only did questions lurk behind his gray eyes, but he had her dreaming of kindness and lovers' touches—things she'd given up on.

She met his direct gaze. "Don't worry about me. I will be fine."

His eyes narrowed a fraction. Once again he was trying to peer into her soul.

Finally he drew back. "If you're not wanted by the law, I guess that means you're a runaway. The question now is who are you running from?"

Her skin itched with fear. "Stay out of my business, Mr. Mitchell."

Ben shoved his hands into his pockets. "I wish that I could." He rose and left the room....

* * *

Heart of the Storm
Harlequin Historical #757—June 2005

Acclaim for Mary Burton's recent works

The Unexpected Wife
"If you liked *Sarah, Plain and Tall,* you'll love this book.
It's a touch different, but alike in all the right places."
—*Romantic Times*

Rafferty's Bride
"Ms. Burton has written a romance filled with passion
and compassion, forgiveness and humor; the kind of
well-written story that truly touches the heart because
you can empathize with the characters."
—*Romantic Times*

The Perfect Wife
"Mary Burton presents an intricate theme that questions
if security rather than attraction defines the basis of
love."
—*Romantic Times*

The Colorado Bride
"This talented writer is a virtuoso, who strums the hearts
of readers and composes an emotional tale.
I was spellbound."
—*Rendezvous*

MARY BURTON

Heart of the Storm

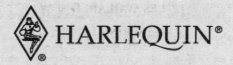

HARLEQUIN®

TORONTO • NEW YORK • LONDON
AMSTERDAM • PARIS • SYDNEY • HAMBURG
STOCKHOLM • ATHENS • TOKYO • MILAN • MADRID
PRAGUE • WARSAW • BUDAPEST • AUCKLAND

ISBN 0-373-29357-7

HEART OF THE STORM

www.eHarlequin.com

Printed in U.S.A.

Available from Harlequin Historicals and
MARY BURTON

A Bride for McCain #502
The Colorado Bride #570
The Perfect Wife #614
Christmas Gold #627
"Until Christmas"
Rafferty's Bride #632
The Lightkeeper's Woman #693
The Unexpected Wife #708
Heart of the Storm #757

Please address questions and book requests to:
Harlequin Reader Service
U.S.: 3010 Walden Ave., P.O. Box 1325, Buffalo, NY 14269
Canadian: P.O. Box 609, Fort Erie, Ont. L2A 5X3

For Elizabeth and Lee

Chapter One

Washington City
March 1866

She couldn't breathe.

Rachel Emmons had never done anything more desperate in her life. She was running away from her husband, Peter Emmons, a man who in a rage had struck her so hard last night that the pins from her chignon had pinged on the Italian marble floor of their Washington town house.

This hadn't been the first beating in their eleven-month marriage, but it had been, by far, the worst.

The early morning air was damp, the fog thick as she hurried down the cobblestone streets past the bales of tobacco, sacks of flour and piles of freshly milled lumber. The Potomac shipyards were busy this morning. Sailors readied their ships, farmers drove their carts filled with produce and men of business inspected cargo. Her heart pounded in her chest as she searched for the *Anna St. Claire.*

She'd dressed in widow's weeds with a heavy lace veil over her hat. Widows were invisible. And she wanted no one to remember her or to see the bruise on her face.

She pushed through the crowds and moved toward the docks. The innkeeper had told her the *Anna St. Claire* would be moored on a pier near the tobacco warehouses. The small freighter was scheduled to leave on the morning tide. But as she made her way through the early morning throng, she saw no sign of the ship. She scanned the vessel nearest her. *The Maria Nova.*

A sailor bumped Rachel's shoulder. She murmured an apology and hurried further down the dock, fearing she'd taken a wrong turn. What if she couldn't find the freighter before it sailed out of port? She clenched her gloved hands. She couldn't go back.

She stepped around a crowd of men, not daring to ask for directions for fear they'd remember her if questioned later. The next ship was a slow draft steamer, the *Zephyr.* Her brisk pace quickened to a run as she headed toward the next set of sails.

To her relief she found the *Anna St. Claire* two blocks north of where the innkeeper had said it would be. The three-masted schooner was weathered and in desperate need of cleaning. Cargo was piled high on the deck and her hull rode low in the water, a sign she was loaded and ready to leave. Her patched sails flapped in the wind.

There were eight men aboard. The sailors who manned this ship were rough, hard-bitten men. Several shouted profanities. One sailor dropped his trousers and urinated over the side of the ship.

Two sailors pointed at her. A redheaded one grabbed his crotch and laughed. "Nay, I can't see her face. But I can tell by her stiff back that she needs a man to loosen her up. She's in need of a good poke."

"Ah, but with a stick like yours, Sebastian," the shorter sailor said, "she'll never know she's been had. She needs a real man, like me."

The men laughed, each going into detail about what they'd do if given an afternoon alone with her in a cabin.

Such indignities would be a part of her new life. But Rachel would pay any price to be free of Peter and her godless marriage.

She could do this.

From the top deck a man shouting orders to his sailors caught her attention. He wore a bright blue coat, black pants, polished knee-high boots and a wide-brimmed hat. A black beard covered his olive-skinned face. Captain Antoine LaFortune. The innkeeper had said LaFortune would give her passage, no questions asked.

Gathering her courage, she climbed the steep, slippery wooden plank and stepped onto the deck. The captain noticed her instantly, his gaze lean and hungry.

The fine Belgium lace of her veil fluttered in the wind and her black wool skirts rustled as she stepped over the thick coiled rope on deck. The ship smelled of tobacco and lumber.

Each man working on deck stopped to watch her as she walked toward the captain. The red-headed sailor grinned at her and licked his lips.

Captain LaFortune climbed down from the upper deck and tugged at the edges of his cuffs. The former blockade-runner's belly was round, straining the buttons on his vest. His face was pock-marked under his beard and he wore his thinning black hair tied at the nape of his neck. *"Bonjour, madame."*

Through her veil she looked up at him. *"Bonjour, monsieur. Captain LaFortune?"*

He grinned, revealing yellowed teeth. *"Oui. Américaine?"*

"Oui."

"I speak English," he said proudly. "How may I be of service to you, my lady?"

Her spine was so straight she imagined it would snap. "I need passage."

He lifted a brow, amused. "I command a freighter, madame. I am an honest businessman who carries lumber, tobacco and wine, not young widows."

She kept her voice even. From what she'd been told, he did most anything if the price was right. "The innkeeper of the Salty Dog on First Street said you carry special passengers from time to time."

His eyes reminded her of black buttons. "Perhaps I do."

Aware that the other sailors could hear, she lowered her voice. "Where are you sailing to on this voyage?"

He leaned a fraction closer. The scent of his unwashed body overpowered her. She wrinkled her nose. "Do I know you, madame?"

Nervously she fingered the lace trimming her reticule. "I don't think so."

Peter, as head of Venture Shipping, was quite well known on the East Coast. He'd made his fortune during the war, trading with the South and the North. Her husband had insisted she always travel with him since they'd married. It was very possible she and LaFortune had crossed paths. Most assuredly, he'd heard of Peter. She prayed he didn't recognize her.

His eyes narrowed. "I think you are wrong, madame. I can't place you now, but it will come to me. I have a very good memory and your voice is quite unique. It reminds me of the women in the Mediterranean."

Her heart raced but she kept her voice even. "Your destination, sir?"

He studied her a moment longer, then shrugged. "To the port of St. Thomas. It can be a rough place for a woman alone."

She was only sorry it wasn't farther away from Washington. "That will do."

His gaze glided up and down her petite frame. "Passage is not cheap."

Rachel had nearly one hundred dollars. Peter rarely had cash in the house but he had set the money aside to buy flowers for their first anniversary party. She'd wedged open his desk with a letter opener and taken the money. "How much?"

As if he read her mind he said, "Two hundred dollars."

"That's triple the going rate of the passenger ships!"

He rubbed the thick black stubble on his chin, no hint of apology in his eyes. "*Oui*, it is."

Rachel's heart sank. It was only a matter of time before Peter found her. He'd be returning to the town house tomorrow or the next day at the latest. She had to leave the country.

Her thoughts turned to her wedding band. Encircled with diamonds and rubies, it was worth a small fortune. She tugged off the glove on her left hand and removed her ring. "This should cover my passage."

The captain took her ring and studied it. He held it up to the light. "It is an exquisite piece of jewelry indeed."

She'd grown to hate the ring and all that it symbolized. "It's one of a kind."

His gaze sharpened with interest. He looked inside the band. "There is an inscription," he said. "Forever and always."

"Yes." On her wedding day when she'd read the words, she'd been touched. Now they haunted her.

He held the ring up so that the sunlight reflected in the gems. "A widow who trades her wedding band must be quite desperate to leave."

Her knees were shaking, but she held her chin high. "Do you accept my offer or not, Captain?"

LaFortune studied the ring a beat longer.

Rachel held her breath.

"Oui," he said finally, tucking the ring into his vest pocket. "How could I resist such a generous offer? Welcome aboard the *Anna St. Claire.*"

His greeting didn't offer much relief. This journey was the first of many to come. She had enough funds to get her through the next few months, but beyond that she didn't know what she was going to do. "Thank you."

The captain glanced around her. "And your bags?"

When she'd left the town house she'd not taken a bag fearing some of the servants loyal to Peter would contact him. She'd told her maid she was going to shop for an anniversary gift for Peter. "I've none."

"And the mystery deepens. So young. No luggage. And a widow. That is regrettable."

"Yes, regrettable."

"Do you have a name, madame?"

"I believe I have just paid for my privacy."

A slow smile curved his lips. *"Oui.* You have. But then we have eight days to get to know one another very well."

Peter had taught her to school her emotions. Though she wanted to run from this vile ship, she held her ground. "We shall see."

The captain signaled his first officer over. The large, heavyset man moved toward them with uncommon agility. "Yes, Captain?"

"Rubin, show madame to my cabin. She will be traveling with us. Mr. Rubin keeps the eight men on this ship in line, including myself sometimes."

Rubin glanced down at her. His gaze traveled over her black dress and veiled face. "A woman is bad luck, but a widow is daring fate to destroy us. The men will not like it."

LaFortune shrugged. "She is paying well."

"We've had smooth sailing since New York," the old sailor said. "Why tempt the seas now? Our lives are not worth whatever fare she has paid."

The captain's smile flattened. "Madame, you must excuse Rubin. He has sailed the seas for over forty years, but he is quite superstitious."

Rachel sensed the power play between the two men. She kept silent.

"Good luck is why I've lived so long," Rubin said.

The captain's gaze hardened.

Rubin wasn't happy, but he knew when he had pushed too far. "Very well. But we will regret this." He nodded toward the small door that led to the hold below. "This way."

As Rachel started to turn, the wind caught her veil and whisked it back off her face. For an instant her gaze caught the captain's. She saw his eyes spark with interest as he studied the bruise marring her left eye. She quickly grabbed the veil and pulled it back in place.

The captain frowned. "Who would mar such a lovely face as yours?"

Rachel held the veil in place with a gloved hand. "It was an accident."

He smiled. "Of course."

He didn't believe her, and she did not care. As long as he didn't press her for details and left her alone, she was satisfied.

She wanted nothing more than to find her cabin and bar the door. "My cabin, Mr. Rubin?"

Nodding, the old sailor led her belowdecks. Rubin had to stoop to move down the low, narrow hallway. The smell of urine and filth, magnified by the confined space, assailed her.

He opened a small door to a cabin. The room had a bunk, one chair and a chamber pot next to the bed. A small portal above the bunk looked out onto the harbor. The precious little floor space was crammed full of crates of wine.

"Will you be needing anything?" Rubin asked.

She stepped into the room. The sheets on the bunk were stained. A rat scurried into a corner then disappeared behind a crate. Eight days in this hole seemed intolerable. However she had no choice.

Choking back her fear she said, "No."

"Then I will leave you."

She stared out the portal onto the busy dock. Hundreds of people milled around out there. The thought that one could be Peter had her itching to leave port. "Mr. Rubin, how long until we sail?"

He stopped, his hand on the door handle ready to close it. "A half hour."

Too long. She would not rest easy until the shores of America were out of sight. "Thank you."

With a grunt, Rubin closed the door behind him.

Rachel sat in the chair. She removed her veil. The air in the cabin was thick, but still it felt good to be free of the suffocating veil. She draped the veil over the back of the chair. She tugged off her second glove and, along with the other, folded it neatly. She took great care to tuck both in her reticule next to her money and a small volume of poems. The task complete, she folded her hands in her lap. She considered reading several poems. They always calmed her. Her stomach already queasy from the rocking of the ship, she decided against it.

The ship creaked. Above, the captain shouted commands.

She caught her reflection in a small mirror nailed to the wall beside the bunk. Her blue eyes were sunken, lifeless, and her skin pale. She looked much older than her twenty-three years.

How had her life become such a terrible mess?

This time last year, everything had been different. Her father had been alive and she'd been the belle of her social circle.

Then her father had died suddenly. Rachel had known Peter, a business associate of her father's, for years. Peter had been a kind, gentle man. And when she'd learned that her father's finances were in a shambles, he'd helped her with the creditors. He was always there. Quiet, ready to help.

So when he'd offered marriage, it had seemed quite natural to say yes. She'd imagined her affection would grow over time and one day she would love Peter.

She'd been such a naive fool.

In the first weeks of their marriage he'd insisted on knowing where she was going. In her father's house, she had had greater freedom than most women and she'd been accustomed to coming and going as she'd pleased. She'd been taken aback by Peter's command at first. But vowing to be a good wife, she'd complied. Then Peter had objected to her friends who'd called on her at her home. She'd accepted that marriage meant change, and though she didn't like it, she'd told her friends not to call. In time, she reasoned, when Peter wasn't under such great pressure at work, he would ease his restriction. However, the rules had only grown stricter. And it wasn't long before her clothes weren't quite right. They were too loud, too bold. Her opinions weren't ladylike.

To keep the peace she'd started to compromise. She wore more somber clothes. She spoke less often and put aside her books.

Soon, Peter saw to it that she never left the house unless he was with her. He chose what she wore, what she ate and when she slept. She'd become a prisoner with only her needlework to occupy her time.

Two nights ago, they'd come home from a party. Peter had been in a rage because she'd talked too long to a young man. He'd accused her of having an affair. Though she'd tried to allay his fears, he'd grown angrier by the moment. And this time he'd hit her.

For the first time she'd seen the true monster that lurked behind the blond hair and blue eyes.

As she'd lain on the cold floor, bruised and bleeding, Rachel had begun to plan her escape.

The next morning, Peter had kissed her on the

cheek and bid her good day. He'd planned to take her on his business trip to Baltimore, but her left eye had been far too black. Her appearance would have raised questions. So he'd been forced to leave her behind. Next time, he'd scolded, she should not make him so angry.

She'd stood at her bedroom window watching him as he'd climbed into his carriage. When the carriage had rounded the corner, she'd fled.

She'd gone to the docks and inquired about freighters that took on passengers. Forced to wait for the morning tide, she'd spent the night in an inn by the docks.

Only a day, two at most, remained before Peter returned. A couple of days to put as much distance as she could between them.

Within a half hour, the *Anna St. Claire* set sail. The trip down the river was smooth. As the hours ticked by, her nerves relaxed a fraction. Everything was going to be fine.

By midafternoon, they reached the waters of the Chesapeake Bay and then the Atlantic. As they turned south and passed the shores of Virginia, the waters became choppy. As they headed out to sea, the waters grew rougher. The freighter's white sails strained in the high winds and her mast creaked and moaned.

The cabin rocked and Rachel found it hard to sit in the chair. Outside, the waves pitched. The sky had grown black. Raindrops covered the glass portal. They were headed into a storm.

Rachel had never been a good sailor, but the constant rocking soon made her seasick. Unable to hold down her food, she found the chamber pot by the bunk and wretched. Unable to sit up any longer, she crawled into the bunk. She loosened the braid coiled at the nape of her neck. Closing her eyes, she tried to sleep.

However, when sleep took her, she dreamed of a monster with glowing red eyes looming in the shadows. The creature moved toward her, one step at a time. Her heart raced. Tears stung her eyes. She knew if he caught her, she'd die.

Pounding on her door had her sitting up. She didn't know how long she'd slept, but the storm was all around them, like a wraith ready to steal their lives.

Weak with nausea, she faced the cabin door. "What's going on?"

Footsteps shuffled outside her door seconds before a hard object hit the hallway floor. Rachel reached for a blanket on the edge of the bed. She pulled it over her shoulders. Her hair brushed her backside.

"The Lord is my shepherd and I shall not want." Rubin's deep voice rushed in under the door.

Pressing her hand to her stomach, she moved across the room, swaying to keep her balance. She opened her cabin door and found Rubin picking up a hammer. In his other hand was a crude crucifix lashed together with rope.

Rubin glanced nervously up at her and then to the stairwell to the upper deck where the storm raged.

"What are you doing?" she demanded.

Hammer in hand, he stood. "I was nailing the cross over your door to break your curse."

Rachel stared into his brown eyes, which were wild with fear. "I've brought no curse on this ship." She tried to move past Rubin.

"Aye, you have. Ol' Nate said we was supposed to have smooth seas all the way. Ol' Nate is never wrong about the weather. You've brought us bad luck."

"I have no control over the weather. You are a fool to think that I do."

Anger mingled with fear in his eyes. "You may have fooled the captain," he snarled, "but not me."

"I want to go on deck and speak to the captain this instant."

Rubin blocked her exit with his large body. He smelled of sweat and fear. "You'll stay right here.

The men are busy lowering the lifeboats and they don't need your curses."

They were abandoning ship and leaving her behind? "I must see the captain."

Rubin folded his arms over his chest. "You'll get no help from him. He's got his hands full keeping this ship afloat."

"Move out of my way. You can't make me stay. I paid good money."

"Dead men can't spend money."

"Get out of my way!" she screamed.

Rubin shoved her into the cabin and closed her door.

In the next instant the ship pitched violently and she stumbled back. She lost her footing. She grabbed onto a chair, but the chair toppled forward under her weight. She fell hard and hit her head against the corner of a wooden crate. Pain registered for only a moment and then her world went black.

When Rachel awoke, she was aware of the howling wind outside. And the cold.

She was lying in two inches of water.

Chapter Two

Rain pelted Ben Mitchell as he rowed toward the wreck of the *Anna St. Claire*.

His assistant, Timothy Scott, sat in front of him in the boat. It was the boy's first sea rescue. He was huddled under his black slicker; a stocking cap covering his red hair. Even over the wind Ben could hear the lad's teeth chattering with fear and cold.

"The freighter is so close, I swear I could spit on her," Timothy said.

"Aye, she's not more than one hundred yards from the shore."

Ben glanced over his shoulder at the schooner. The right side of her hull had sunk so low that stormy waves washed over her bow. The ship's masts were broken and her torn white sails flapped in the wind like eerie specters.

Timothy gripped the side of the dory. "Are the wrecks always so close?"

Ben dug the oars into the water. "No. We're lucky this time."

"*Luck.*" The boy laughed. "Only a keeper would be talking of luck while rowing out to a wreck in this kind of weather."

"Wait until the day you row out a half mile to a ship in weather worse than this." This past winter had been one of the worst on the outer banks. The nor'easters had fooled many a ship's captain. There'd been more wrecks than normal and the bodies of dozens of unnamed sailors had washed up on the beaches. He'd be glad to see spring.

The lighthouse beacon blinked steady and bright as the seas caught the dory and dragged her further out to sea. The riptide would make getting back to shore more difficult than he'd first thought. But there was no worrying about that when there will was a ship to board and search.

Ben had served as lightkeeper for six months. He'd been hired late last fall as the Winter Man, a temporary replacement to fill the shoes of the old keeper who had died suddenly. After twelve years in the Navy and an unexpected discharge, he'd come home to visit his aunt and cousin.

Ben had been at loose ends. He'd had offers

from several shipping companies, but he had lost his taste for sailing the seas.

The short-term job as winter man had suited him for the time being. Two weeks ago, he'd received a letter from the Life Saving Service. The board had offered him the position full-time. He'd yet to give his answer.

The service had hired Timothy less than a month ago in the hope that the extra help would entice Ben to stay. Timothy had been raised in a family of fisherman who worked the waters off the outer banks. Though Ben thought the boy talked too much, he understood the ocean and the dangers of the Graveyard's waters. Whether Ben stayed or left, Timothy would serve well.

"Why didn't the ship's captain heed the flare you fired?" Timothy asked, shouting over the wind.

"Who's to say?" Ben dug his oars deeper into the water. He'd fired flares from his Costen gun several times when he'd first spied the ship, but the captain had not altered his course. Ego, pride or most likely the captain had already abandoned the ship. He'd find out soon enough.

The two lapsed into silence as Ben dug the boat oars into the water and drove them toward the freighter.

Within minutes the dory skimmed the side of

the boat just below a burnished sign that read *Anna St. Claire.* "Take the oars, Timothy. Hold her steady while I go aboard to see if there's anyone left to save."

Relief washed over Timothy's face as he scooted forward and took the oars. "I don't mind coming with you, sir."

Ben had enough trouble on his hands without the worry of a green lad traipsing about a dying vessel. "Stay put and keep the dory steady."

Waves crashed into the side of the rowboat. Cold rain drizzled. Timothy didn't offer an argument.

Ben wiped the rain from his face. He grabbed a rope dangling from the side of the ship. He tugged on it to make sure it was secure.

"Ben, do you really have to board her? The ship looks abandoned. It's like the ghost tales I've heard the seamen tell."

Superstition was as much a part of this region and the wind and sea, but Ben had little patience for talk of ghosts and curses. It had been his experience that trouble was caused by the living not the dead. "There're no ghosts aboard this vessel."

Timothy stared up at the shadowy vessel. "Yeah, but what if there are ghosts and they are watching us now? Sends a shiver down my spine."

A slight smile tipped the edge of Ben's mouth. "That's the icy waters, lad, not ghosts."

Ben gripped the rope and, using it as balance, scaled up the side of the ship. He swung his leg over the ship's railing and landed on the deck. It listed beneath his weight.

The center mast had cracked two thirds of the way up and fallen into the ocean. The other sails were torn and flapping wildly in the storm. Wind scattered the ropes and crates over the deck.

"Can you see anything?" Timothy shouted.

The rain blew sideways, stinging Ben's face as he started his search. "No. Not yet. Hand me up the lantern."

Timothy moved to the edge of the dory and on wobbly legs handed the lantern up to Ben.

Ben cursed the wind that made the light flicker and spit. Protecting the flame with his body, he turned up the wick.

The lantern light cast an eerie glow on the ship. A quick survey revealed that Timothy had been right. All the lifeboats were gone. A closer inspection of the top deck confirmed there wasn't a sign of any soul. Likely, the men had fled the vessel when the main mast had started to go.

No doubt the sailors would turn up somewhere along the outer banks, either dead or alive. The chances of finding any survivors on the *Anna St. Claire* looked slim.

But Ben was thorough.

He'd learned that perception and fact didn't always agree. So he would search this vessel, and only when he'd confirmed with his own two eyes that she had been abandoned, would he leave.

He moved to the ship's railing and called down to Timothy. "If I'm not back in ten minutes, leave."

"Where are you going?" Timothy shouted over the wind. He huddled in the boat, his hands wrapped around his body.

"Belowdecks."

"The lifeboats are gone, Ben. The sailors have all abandoned ship. Give up the search."

"I'll make a quick check belowdecks before I write this ship off." His tenacity served him well. It had also led to his court-martial. *What made you great was your undoing,* the admiral had said to him. "Remember, if I'm not back in ten, leave."

Timothy wiped water from his face. "I won't leave without you."

"You just celebrated your twentieth birthday and you and Callie are to wed in less than a week. Ten minutes, Tim, and I expect you to start rowing."

Just then the freighter shifted, pitching Ben forward. He nearly dropped the lantern. Wood splintered and cracked somewhere on the vessel. He gripped the railing, his muscles bunching under his thick cable-knit sweater and dark jacket. His iron grip kept him from falling headfirst into the ocean. The lantern light nearly went out.

Timothy's face was pale and panicked in the lantern light. "Please, sir, give it up. The ship is going to break up."

Water dripped from his nose as Ben glared down at his assistant. "Ten minutes."

Without another word, he strode across the badly sloping deck. By the time he reached the hatchway that led below, rainwater had drenched his black pea coat. Turning the knob, he shoved open the hatch.

He held up the light. Three feet of black ocean water lapped against the third rung of the ladder. Outside the wind howled.

"Hello down there!" he called. Silence.

Debris floated past three doorways that fed into the hallway. Two on the left and one on the right.

Seconds passed as he strained to hear. "Hello!" he shouted again. Nothing.

Perhaps Timothy was right.

Everyone was gone or dead.

Ben turned on the ladder ready to climb above deck when he heard the muffled scream. At first he thought it was a trick of the wind.

But he stopped and listened. The wail returned, sounding more human—and more feminine—than before. But a woman aboard a freighter didn't make sense.

"Hello down there," he shouted.

The screaming stopped and for a moment there was only silence. Then he heard, "Is someone out there?"

The woman's voice was unmistakable.

"Yes! I'm here," he shouted.

"Thank God! Please help me."

"Where are you?"

"I'm in the cabin on the right." Her voice sounded broken, as if she'd been sobbing. "They locked me in."

Ben raised the lantern and looked around for something he could use to break the door. He spotted an ax hanging on a wall by the stairs.

Ben grabbed the ax off its peg, hung the lantern in its place and climbed down the ladder. Raising the ax high over his head, he started to wade into the hallway. The eerie creaks and sways of the dying ship echoed around him. "I'm coming for you."

The woman began to pound her door harder. "Hurry, the cabin is filling with water."

Ben pushed past the floating debris. His limbs

tingled from the cold. He tried the knob on the door. It was indeed locked.

"Please don't leave me." The woman's desperation punctuated every syllable.

"I'm not going anywhere without you."

"What can I do to help?"

"Step back," Ben shouted. "I'll have to cut my way through the door.

He heard the splash of water. "I'm away from the door."

Ben's shoulders ached and the weight of his damp clothes made it nearly impossible for him to raise his arms over his head in the narrow hallway. It was only a matter of minutes before he'd lose feeling in his feet in the cold waters.

The lantern swayed and flickered in the wind behind him. Gritting his teeth, he jerked the ax back an extra inch then drove it with every bit of force left in his body. The blade sliced through the door as if it were butter. Ben yanked the ax free and drove it again into the door. Soon the door snapped in two.

Immediately water from the hallway rushed into the cabin. He heard the woman scream. Dropping the ax, he bolted into the darkened cabin.

The river of seawater knocked Rachel off balance. She tumbled backward. Salt water filled her mouth and nose as her arms flayed around. She didn't know what was up or down as she groped wildly for something to grab onto.

For all her desperate plans of escape, she feared she was going to die. Peter would have smiled at the irony. He'd always said he'd kill her if she tried to leave.

Strong hands banded around her arms and hauled her forward above the surface of the water. She sucked in a breath.

Her eyes burning, she stared at the silhouette of a very large man. Hints of lantern light from the hallway flickered on chiseled features and black eyes.

The cold had seeped through her dress and sapped her strength. Her teeth chattered. Her hair, in a long thick plait down her back, draped over her shoulder like a wet rope.

"Is there anyone else?" His voice was deep, rusty and full of authority.

"I don't think so. I heard them lower the lifeboats hours ago. I screamed but no one came."

The man muttered a savage oath. The boat shifted then, knocking her off balance and into his chest. Warmth and energy radiated from him. And for just the faintest moment she felt safe.

His strong fingers gripped her arm and he pushed her toward the door. "Let's go," he ordered.

"We don't have much time before she's completely flooded."

Wading across the tiny room in waist-deep water and then down the hallway took every ounce of strength left in Rachel's body. The weight of her skirts added to the burden of every step.

When they reached the ladder leading to the deck above, the boat tilted and groaned again. Water rushed down the ladder. She fell back into the stranger.

He wrapped strong fingers around her shoulders. "Move, or we both will die here," he growled in her ear.

He placed his hands around her narrow waist and propelled her forward through the icy waterfall. The thick wool of her dress was completely soaked and it clung to her body like a second skin.

Rachel coughed as she stumbled forward to the upper deck. She sucked in a deep breath.

The rain had slowed. In the distance she saw the lighthouse beacon. There, she'd be safe. But it was so far away.

The deck above was sloping badly now, and each time she tried to stand, her foot caught in her drenched hem. The stranger grabbed her elbow and jerked her up.

"I can't walk. My skirts are so heavy." Lord,

but she sounded weak. The cold night air pricked her skin.

"We're almost there." Urgency laced each word. "Just a few more yards."

She forced herself to remain standing. "I am not going to die now. I've come *too far.* I've come too far." She hadn't realized she'd chanted the words out loud until he spoke.

"Aye, we've both come too far to die now." He pushed his shoulder into her midsection and lifted her up off the ground. His shoulder dug into her belly and she could barely breathe.

He dashed across the deck until he reached the railing.

She caught a glimpse of the ocean below. A small boat bobbed in the water. The black seas churned.

She gripped his wet coat with her frozen fingers. "I can't swim!" she shouted.

"I can."

He tossed her over the side of the railing into the churning waters.

Chapter Three

Rachel's sense of weightlessness lasted only an instant. Before she could scream, she landed in the water.

The icy ocean engulfed her mouth and nose as she plowed downward through the water. Her blood thrummed with fear.

For one heart-stopping moment she thought she'd never reach air again. She tasted salt. Her lungs ached and burned.

She clawed her way through the water, wondering what she'd do if she reached the surface. Even if she hadn't had the heavy skirts weighing her down, she couldn't swim.

A strong hand grabbed her forearm and hauled her upward. She clung to her rescuer, knowing without him she'd die. She broke through the water's edge and sucked in a huge breath, coughing. Her bare shoulder bumped against something hard and she realized she'd been pushed beside a rowboat.

"Steady the oars, Timothy," her rescuer said. "I've got a woman." The confidence in his voice relaxed her. Somehow she knew she was safe.

He wrapped his hands around her waist, holding her body close to his. "Hold on to the boat's edge. I'm going to climb in and pull you aboard."

She panicked. "Don't leave me."

He moved so close that his lips were right next to her ear. "Be brave. I'll have you in the boat in a second."

Her skin burned in the ice-cold water. She could barely hold on to the slick lip of the boat as it was. But when she looked into his warm, steady gaze she knew he wouldn't leave her. "Hurry."

Her rescuer easily swung his long legs over the side of the boat. The boat dipped and swayed but he steadied himself as if he were on dry land.

He leaned over the edge and, grabbing her arms, pulled her up into the boat and eased her to the bottom. A bone-deep cold had settled into her body. Her teeth chattered.

"Where'd you find her?" the young man said, handing a blanket to her rescuer.

"Belowdecks." He wrapped the blanket around her. The coarse fabric offered some warmth, but she couldn't shake the chill.

The boy looked at her as if she were a specter. "In a million years, I never would have guessed there'd be a woman aboard that freighter."

The man sat behind her, bracing his feet on either side of her. Powerful thighs rubbed her shoulders. "That's the key, lad. Never guess."

"Yes, sir."

"Timothy, get another blanket for the woman." He took hold of the oars and started to row. The boat started toward the shore.

"Anything you say, Mr. Mitchell." The younger man took his place, reached behind him and produced a thick wool blanket from under a tarp.

Timothy handed Rachel the blanket and she wasted no time wrapping it around her shoulders.

Mr. Mitchell. Her savior had an ordinary name, she thought absently as she managed to sit up on the boat bottom. The heroes in the books she read always seemed to have such exotic, memorable names.

She hugged her arms over her wet shoulders, unsure if she should be grateful or sick to her stomach.

Mr. Mitchell dug the oars into the water. The boat started to glide. How he had the energy to row was beyond her comprehension.

Strength radiated from his body. Such power, she'd learned, gave him complete control over her. The man had just saved her life and already suspicion clouded her thoughts of him. Marriage to Peter had done that.

The name was ordinary, but the man was not.

Mr. Mitchell was dirty, covered in sand and seaweed, yet unlike the sailors on the ship, there wasn't the stench of rotting teeth or filth about him. Instead he possessed a musky kind of man smell that intrigued her.

She closed her eyes. Lord, but she was tired of being afraid. She wanted her life back. She wanted to laugh again.

But she was so cold. And so very tired. She simply wanted to sleep now. Exhausted, she leaned to the left. Her cheek brushed Mr. Mitchell's thigh.

"What's your name?" Mr. Mitchell said.

His gruff voice startled her. She opened her eyes and sat up straight, suddenly aware that she'd laid her cheek against his thigh. "It's Rachel."

"You have a last name?" he said.

She hesitated. Peter would return to Washington soon. And he'd be looking for her. "Davis. Rachel Davis." The surname belonged to her maid.

"Where are you from?"

She didn't want to talk. She was so tired and cold she could barely string two thoughts together.

He stared down at her unsmiling. Lantern light deepened the hard planes of his face. She feared for one moment that he had the power to read into her soul.

"What were you doing on the *Anna St. Claire?*"

"I've family in the Caribbean." She hated lying, but trust was a luxury she couldn't afford.

The boat rose and fell with the tides. His thigh brushed her shoulder. "Most women don't travel freighters."

"It was economical." *And very expedient.*

Tension tightened the muscles in his body, as if he sensed she was lying. "I see."

She suppressed a shiver, telling herself it was the cold. The rain had slowed but the night air cut through her drenched gown. Rachel longed to escape this boat and Mr. Mitchell's scrutiny. "I owe you my thanks, sir."

He shrugged. "It's what I do."

"You're lucky Ben was on duty," Timothy said rubbing his hands together for warmth. "Not all keepers would fight the surf as he does."

She glanced at the boy. About her age, yet he looked so young. Or was it that she just felt so old?

Her teeth started to chatter and her hands to

shake. Mr. Mitchell tightened his legs around her shoulders, giving her his warmth.

She shifted, uncomfortable with the contact.

"You're freezing. My legs will keep you warmer."

"I'm fine," she said.

"You're blue."

Unconsciously her fingers curled into fists, ready to fight if need be. Her days of giving in were over. "The blankets will warm me soon enough."

"You must put your modesty aside, Mrs. Davis, until you are warm. The cold can take your life as easily as the ocean."

Mrs. Davis. He'd called her Mrs. Davis. He'd not looked past her widow's weeds. Good.

She forced herself to relax, which was hard because her teeth were chattering. However, she did see the wisdom of his words. She'd die if she didn't get warm. "You're right of course. I—I'm being silly."

"No problem."

She adjusted the blanket so that it covered her shoulders. He tightened his legs around her. The warmth of his body lulled her closer.

She should have been relieved, but she wasn't. Depending on anyone was simply too dangerous.

* * *

Davis. As common a name as there was for a woman who looked anything but common.

The woman's body felt fragile against Ben's thighs. Her thick tangle of hair had escaped its braid and hung freely down her back, skimming the middle of her backside. He imagined when dry it shone like gold and felt like down. Her fine-boned features were ghostly pale now, but warmth, time and a few good meals would make her stunning.

As he held her against him, he was very aware of the full curve of her breasts rubbing his thigh. He imagined the ripeness of her nipples straining against the wet fabric, and the narrow curve of her hips.

Again she laid her head on his leg. She was falling asleep. In this cold, that wasn't good.

"Where is your husband?" he said, determined to keep her talking.

Startled, she opened her eyes. Confusion and fear flashed in their blue depths before they cleared. She shifted her gaze out to the sea. "He's dead."

"How long?"

"Not long."

The news should have meant nothing to him. Widow or married, it shouldn't matter either way to him.

But it did.

He waited for her to elaborate, but she didn't.

Her silence spoke volumes.

Ben frowned. It wasn't simply the cold that was affecting her now.

Rachel Davis was hiding something.

The tide had been more brutal than Mr. Mitchell had first thought. He told Timothy as much when he'd ordered him to the oars. The boy had taken his place by Ben and together they rowed to shore. It seemed there was a time or two that Mr. Mitchell and Timothy looked worried.

However, fifteen minutes later, the boat bottom scraped the sand. The rain had all but stopped, the heavy winds had thinned and the thick clouds had parted. Moonlight shone down on the beach and the dunes.

The wind sliced through her wet clothes like a knife. Rachel feared she'd never be warm again.

She sat up, pulling free of Mr. Mitchell's embrace. "Where are we?"

"Off the coast of North Carolina, Mrs. Davis," he said. "Between Corolla and Hatteras." He rose. "Stay put. I'll be back."

Leaving her, he climbed out of the boat. Immediately she missed the heat of his body.

Mr. Mitchell grabbed the side of the boat.

Waves crashed around his feet. His biceps bunched and corded muscles in his neck strained as he and Timothy yanked the boat ashore.

Her mind, befuddled by the cold, marveled that Mr. Mitchell could stand so tall and strong after such an exhausting rescue. The fact that he could pull the heavy boat ashore was nothing short of a miracle. The man's tenacity simply wasn't human.

She glanced up and down the long beaches that stretched and curved into the horizon. She could make out the outline of the dunes topped with sea oats that swayed in the wind. There wasn't a soul to be found in either direction.

Hundreds of miles separated this isolated land from Peter and Washington, but she feared it wasn't enough. His reach could be quite far.

Her stomach tightened, warning her that she'd have to move on soon. She closed her eyes and tried to calm her racing heart.

"I'll put the boat up, Ben," the young man said. "And I'll take the rest of tonight's shift."

"Thanks." Mr. Mitchell walked over to her and held out his hand. "Ready to go, Mrs. Davis?"

Automatically she rose and took his hand. Steady, warm fingers closed around her hand.

Yet despite her best efforts to stand tall, she started to crumble. Her legs wobbled under the weight of her skirts and her head began to spin. Fisting her hand around the blanket, she drew in deep breaths, trying to will her body to move.

Heavy hands cupped her shoulders. "I've got you." He lifted her out of the boat.

She leaned into him. If she could just rest a moment and catch her breath. "I can't stay here. I have to leave. Is there a town nearby where I can buy clothes?"

A humorless smile tipped the edges of his mouth. "Lady, you're not going anywhere."

Rachel's head spun and her stomach churned. "I have to go."

"Let me help you," he whispered against her ear.

Lord, but she was a pitiable creature. She glared up at him. A grim smile lifted the edge of his lips. She was aware that Timothy was also staring at her. "I need to go."

"Where?" he demanded.

"South."

His gaze grew serious. "Is there someone ex pecting you?"

Hunting me. "No."

"Then give up the fight for tonight. Your skin is like ice. I've a warm bed at the lightkeeper's cottage. Tomorrow you can leave."

The offer was tempting. To wrap herself in the

dry comfort of a bed and let sleep take her for just a little while. But a little rest could cost her her life. "I need to go."

He loosened his hold, a clear sign he'd not argue with her.

Rachel staggered over the uneven sand for several feet. Her fingers ached with cold and fatigue. The added exertion of walking on sand sent her heart pounding and soon her body began to perspire. Her head spun faster and her mouth began to sweat.

Humiliation welled as she realized she was going to throw up in front of this man. She dropped to her knees. She threw up bile.

Mr. Mitchell knelt beside her. He held her hair back from her face and patiently waited until the spasms stopped. "Better?"

She didn't dare raise her eyes to look at him. "Yes."

"It's the middle of the night, Mrs. Davis. You can't go anywhere until morning. Let's get you up to the cottage." He scooped her in his arms and carried her over the dunes.

Rachel didn't argue this time. She was so cold, she couldn't think. But wrapped in his musky, very male scent, she felt safe and protected.

Tomorrow, she'd leave.

For now, all she wanted to do was to sleep.

* * *

Ben was losing Rachel.

The woman he'd battled so hard to save from the doomed *Anna St. Claire* was slipping deeper and deeper into a sleep borne not of fatigue but of a bone-chilling cold that was robbing her of her life. He shifted her in his arms.

She weighted no more than a sack of feathers. Her breathing was rapid and uneven.

Ben glanced at his assistant. "Timothy, I've got to get her inside. The cold is killing her."

"Aye, sir."

"Get yourself into dry clothes and grab something to eat before you head back to the light."

Timothy's shoulders slumped with fatigue. "Aye, sir."

Ben marched up over the dunes and across the sandy yard toward the white lightkeeper's cottage.

Timothy headed into the base of the lighthouse as Ben climbed the stairs of the cottage. The keeper's cottage with its red-tiled roof and large front porch was split into two sections—the larger quarters reserved for the lightkeeper and the smaller one for his assistant.

He pushed open the front door with his wet booted foot. The house was dark and very cold. He was so familiar with the interior that he didn't need a light to know his way. To his right was a parlor. The room was filled with boxes of his belongings. He'd never taken the time to unpack. Beyond the parlor was a large kitchen. He'd made a few unappetizing meals in the kitchen but, like the parlor, the room went unused. He was simply too exhausted after long shifts in the lighthouse to sit and read, let alone cook. Now that Timothy was on board, his long hours would ease. Soon his life would find more balance.

Ben moved purposefully toward the back room. What Rachel needed was a hot bath to warm her bones, but heating water would take more than an hour. He glanced down at her pale skin. Her lips had taken on a blue hue.

Hypothermia.

He moved down the darkened center hallway past two more doors—bedrooms he never used—to his own at the end.

The woman moaned softly. Her fingers were bunched into small fists. No bigger than a sprite, she possessed a warrior spirit he had to admire.

Her face nestled in the crook under his chin. He could feel her warm breath against his skin.

Ben laid her gently on the bed. She rolled onto her side and curled her legs close to her body. She still clutched the blanket close.

He lit a lantern. A soft glow of light shone on the double bed, dresser, sea trunk and large hearth.

He quickly removed his wet jacket and tossed it into a heap on the floor.

Ben turned his attention to Rachel and her damp clothes. She whimpered when he pried the blanket from her hands. "You'll be warm in a minute."

He quickly undressed her. Try as he might, he couldn't ignore the softness of her skin or the ripe fullness of her breasts. He covered her with the thick bedspread. She shivered and burrowed deeper. Lantern light cast a soft glow on her skin.

Ben set to work on lighting a fire. It didn't take long before the wood took flame.

The woman's breathing sounded more labored now, and though the blaze was slowly warming the room, she still trembled under the blankets.

Ben opened the chest at the foot of the bed and removed another blanket. He laid it over her, tucking the edges around her slender frame.

She moaned and rolled onto her other side. "I'm so cold."

Ben touched her forehead. Cold as ice.

He sat on the edge of the bed and uncovered her feet. She moaned in protest until he cupped them between his hands. Slowly her feet warmed.

Warming her with the blankets would take hours.

Accepting what must be, he stripped completely and climbed into the bed. He pulled her cold, naked body against his, tugged the blankets over them and draped his arm across her very narrow waist.

She'd not die on his watch.

Chapter Four

Ben awoke with a start.

His mind fogged with sleep, he thought for a moment he was still a decorated naval officer in command of twenty-six sailors and destined to rise higher through the ranks.

As much as he wanted to believe he was on the clipper ship *Intercept,* reason whispered he couldn't be. Absent were the sway of the ship and the sound of men working. And when had he fallen asleep? He'd never slept the night through when he was at sea.

He sat up and shoved his hands through his hair. Morning sunlight streamed into the cold room through the window by his bed. Outside the wind banged a shutter open and closed. Gradually his mind cleared. He wasn't on his ship. He was in the lightkeeper's cottage.

Ben relaxed back against the pillow. A flock of seagulls squawked outside his window. He glanced over at the hearth to the dying embers.

His senses kicked into play. The *Anna St. Claire* had wrecked. The rescue. He remembered.

He looked down at the woman beside him. Curled on her side, she lay naked under the blankets, her long hair flowing down her back.

Rachel.

The coarse blankets covered her petite frame and molded to the gentle curve of her hip. Her profile was classic, a long patrician nose, high cheekbones and full, round lips. Her skin was the color of porcelain. Beautiful. Her hair, dry now, glistened. He captured a stray curl between his fingers. Silk.

She stirred, stretching her legs. Her bare toes peaked out from the end of the blankets into the morning cold. But they retreated under the blankets and rubbed against his, seeking warmth.

The touch was innocent enough and yet it possessed an intimacy that unsettled him. In the quiet morning hours this was the kind of moment a husband and his wife shared before the day began.

She nestled her bottom closer to him. He grew

as hard as a pike. It had been a long time since he'd had a woman and he was accurately aware of it now.

Of course, if Rachel were his, he'd be under the covers with her. And he'd be kissing her awake as he moved inside her.

Embarrassed by the direction of his thoughts, Ben lay very still, waiting as she settled. She sighed and burrowed her face into her pillow.

He didn't want to wake her. She needed her sleep and, in truth, he liked being close to her. He liked it too damn much.

Taking in a deep breath, he stared out the window. He had no rights to the desires flooding his veins. She'd said her husband was dead, but she could very well have children and a whole other life waiting for her return.

Chance had brought her to these shores, but she would soon leave. She didn't belong here.

He shifted his thoughts to the work to be done today—the ropes to be rewound, the oil that would have to be hauled up the one hundred plus steps of the lighthouse and the lenses that would have to be polished. When that didn't ease the throbbing in his groin, he thought about the frigid waters of the Atlantic. If only he could dip into those waters now.

Rachel stirred and muttered something in her sleep. She rolled onto her back, revealing the other side of her face. In the morning light, he saw the bruise. Angry and purple, it marred an otherwise flawless face. He'd not noticed it last night in the dark.

A primitive anger stirred inside him. Had the sailors done this to her?

Suspicion replaced desire. A woman of means, bruised and traveling alone on a frigate manned by hardened sailors. Nothing about Rachel Davis made sense.

Restless now, he eased up and leaned against the headboard. He'd serve them both well by getting dressed and giving her privacy. When she woke, she'd likely be confused and dazed as most near victims of the sea were.

Later he would talk to her and find out where she came from.

"Ben!" His aunt Ida's voice echoed through his cottage. Ida had taken him in and raised him as her own after his parents had drowned crossing the Sound when he was six. Whenever news of shipwreck reached the nearby village she came to check on him the next morning.

Very aware of his and Rachel's nudity, and the picture they made, Ben vaulted out of bed toward a small dresser. He stumbled over their wet clothes entwined in a sopping mess on the floor.

"Mama, I want to check on Timothy to see if he's doing all right." The voice of Ben's cousin Callie drifted through the small house.

"Not until you've paid your respects to your cousin first. Ben! Are you home? It's Ida and Callie." His aunt's voice grew closer.

"Hello, Ben," Callie said.

He yanked open a dresser drawer and pulled out a pair of dry pants. Their timing was flawless. "I'll be right there."

He yanked the pants up over his hips. As he fumbled with the thirteen buttons on the dual front flaps, Rachel awoke with a start. She sat up in bed, her eyes wild and full of fear.

Her gaze drifted over to him, taking in his naked chest and his half-buttoned pants.

Before he could explain, she scrambled out of the bed, dragging the sheet with her. She scurried into a corner and screamed.

The piercing sound no doubt had been heard thirty miles down the beach at Manteo. Certainly, Ida and Callie had heard it. Damn.

Ben fumbled with his buttons and moved toward Rachel. "Rachel, do you remember me?"

Her doe eyes wide, with panic, stared back at him. White-blond hair streamed over hands that clutched her sheet.

She shook her head and tried to retreat another step. She bumped into the wall.

"Ben!" Ida shouted. "What the devil is going on in there? We heard a woman scream."

Shoving out a breath, he reached for Rachel as if handling a skittish horse. "It's okay. You are safe. I won't hurt you."

She shrank back.

He recoiled his hand. Whoever had hit her had marked her with more than bruises.

"It's all right," he said. "I saved you. Remember? Your ship, the *Anna St. Claire,* sank."

She dragged a shaking hand through her hair and straightened her slumped shoulders. "I remember the cold water." Her husky voice was barely a whisper.

"Aye, it was cold. Your skin was like ice when I carried you here." He swept his arm over the room. "This place…it's the lightkeeper's cottage. You're in my room. *I'm* the lightkeeper."

Flushed cheeks made her blue eyes all the more vivid. She conjured images in his mind of sirens and sea nymphs destined to tempt sailors into dangerous, uncharted waters. The memory of her soft flesh pressed against him this morning still hammered his senses. His arousal hardened against his sloppily buttoned breeches.

There was a hard knock at his door. "Benjamin!"

Double damn. Ben moved to the door and blocked it with his body. "Just a minute."

Rachel glanced down at her sheet-clad body. "I'm naked."

"Your clothes were soaked, draining the heat from your body. You'd developed hypothermia. I took your dress off so you'd be warm. Even with the fire and blankets you were still so cold. That's why I stripped and got into bed with you. For the body heat alone."

She studied him, clearly not trusting him.

"Look, your clothes are still in a cold heap on the floor along with my clothes. I nearly tripped over them just a moment ago."

"Benjamin David Mitchell," Ida said just outside his door. "Your cousin and I are coming in, *now!*" The doorknob turned.

"Just a *minute!*" he shouted. He leaned against the door.

Rachel's gaze darted like a caged animal's. "Who is that shouting?"

"That's my aunt and her daughter, my cousin. They're good women. Nosy, but good."

The door opened a crack. He shoved it closed.

"We don't mean to disturb, Ben, but we heard a scream," Callie said.

Ben shrugged. "There's no keeping them out."

Rachel jerked the edges of the sheet around her. "I need clothes!"

"Do you have that Phoebe from Corolla in there?" Ida said. "She's had her eye on you for months. Lord knows, the woman is known for her dramatics."

"Phoebe is on the mainland, Mama," Callie said. "I bet it's Sara Plank he's got in there."

His aunt and cousin were discussing the intimate details of his life. The day was getting better and better.

Ben shoved out another breath. "There's no avoiding Ida and Callie." He stepped back from the door and opened it.

Ida and Callie burst through the door as Rachel turned her face slightly so that her hair hid her bruise.

She was ashamed of the bruise. The realization dug in his gut.

Ida's silver hair caught the morning light as she stood in stunned silence, a basket of muffins clutched in her hands. Callie's brown eyes, like her mother's, looked surprised as she studied Rachel.

Each woman wore a simple gray wool dress. Ida was the shorter of the two. Callie's body was trim and supple whereas childbirth and the years had left Ida's plump.

"I know every woman on the banks and I've never seen her before," Ida said.

Normally, Ida would have offered him one of her muffins the instant she saw him. He never ate enough for her task. This time, she held on to her basket with a white-knuckled grip.

"Your timing is bad," he said more gruffly than he'd intended.

"Don't you growl at me, Ben Mitchell," Ida said. "What are you about?"

"This isn't what you think," he said, softening his tone.

Ida's and Callie's gazes darted between him and Rachel. Their tight-lipped expressions challenged him.

Ida's grip on the basket was firm. "We understand a man alone has…well, *needs,* but bringing a woman here isn't discreet, Benjamin."

Ben prayed for patience. The last thing he wanted to do was to discuss his *needs* with his aunt. "You've got it wrong, Ida."

"What would the people in the village say?" Callie countered.

"I could give a tinker's damn what they think," he snapped.

Ida wiped a wisp of gray hair off her face. "Language, Benjamin. And you're still the winter man in the Service's eyes. They'd not have offered you the position in the first place if not for the admiral's kind words. And they'll surely withdraw their offer if they get the breath of scandal."

His lips flattened. "I've weathered scandal before."

Ida's eyes softened a fraction. "That was a long time ago."

A year wasn't a long time ago.

Aware of Rachel's presence, he halted the direction of this conversation. In the best of times, he didn't like discussing his past.

He heaved a sigh. "Rachel, this is my aunt, Ida, and my cousin Callie." It annoyed him that his aunt had the power to make him feel like an errant schoolboy. Damn it all, he'd done nothing wrong. "Ladies, I'd like you to meet Rachel Davis. She's from the shipwreck."

"From last night?" Callie said. "Oh, my. Dear, you were on the *Anna St. Claire?*"

Rachel faced them. "Yes."

Ida frowned as she got her first look at Rachel's bruised eye. "Benjamin how did that woman get that bruise on her eye?"

"From the wreck," he said quickly. "She stumbled into a door."

He glanced at Rachel. She stood tall and

proud. Intelligence sparked in her blue eyes. Judging by the bruise's color, it was several days old. She'd gotten it before she'd boarded the vessel.

Ida wasn't buying Ben's story. "The tales I've heard report that the shipwreck was a freighter. What would a woman like you be doing on a freighter?"

Rachel leaned heavily against the wall. "I was traveling south."

Ben wanted to know more, but for now would let the questions alone. She looked ready to collapse. As much as he wanted to scoop her up and tuck her into bed, he didn't want her screaming again. "Her destination is none of our business."

Ida fisted her hands and planted them on her hips. "It's a fair question. You have a right to know who you bring into your house."

Ben glowered at his aunt. "She's not up to the questions now."

Ida shrugged and had the good sense to know when she pushed too far. "All right, she's from the wrecked ship and why she was on such a ship or why she has a bruised face is none of our business. That doesn't explain why she's naked in *your* bed."

He straightened his shoulders. If anyone else had asked him that question, he'd have tossed them out of his house without explanation. But Ida wasn't anyone.

"We came ashore well past midnight," he said.

"Was Timothy with you?" Callie said.

"Aye, and he did a fine job. He's in the lighthouse now."

Callie smiled. "Mama, I want to go see him."

"Wait," Ida said sharply. "And what happened next, Benjamin?"

"She was too cold to make the trip into the village," Ben said. "Otherwise I'd have boarded her at Mae's Inn like I do all the other survivors."

Callie nodded to Ben's pants. "Fix your buttons. They're crooked."

He glanced down. He buttoned the flaps so quickly he was off by two buttonholes on the right side. Irritated, he refastened them. "She was cold and in danger of dying. I got into bed with her to warm her."

Ida lifted a brow.

Callie shrugged. "She was cold, Mama."

Ida glared at the seventeen-year-old.

"Look, there's nothing to worry about," Ben said. "The lady's honor is intact."

Ida folded her arms over her chest—a clear signal that his answer didn't suffice. "I'd like a word with your guest."

"Ida." He shoved out a breath. "Can't it wait?"

Ida stepped around Ben. "When will you be leaving?" she demanded of Rachel.

"Ida, the questions can wait." He laid his hands on her shoulders, ready to turn her toward the door.

Ida pursed her lips, holding steady. "If you are smart, you'll report the wreck and be done with Rachel Davis. You've saved her life—your obligation has been met."

Rachel clutched her sheet. "She is right. I should be leaving," she said.

Ben's gaze pinned Rachel. She looked paler now. "Stay put."

Callie folded her arms over her chest. "Mama, this is Ben you are talking to. He's not good at walking away from unfinished business."

"Well, maybe it's time he learned," Ida snapped.

Callie was right. There were too many questions that needed answering before he walked away from Rachel. He should. But he wouldn't. "She stays until she's strong enough to travel."

"Then bundle her up and send her to my place," Ida said. "I'll care for her."

"The last thing she needs is a mile-long walk in cold morning air," Ben said. "She can barely stand."

"It's not proper," Ida said.

"It's practical," Ben said.

Callie stepped around her mother and extended her hand to Rachel. "Ben will take good care of you. But if there is anything you need, send Ben to the village. Mama and I will help you."

Rachel slowly loosened one white-knuckled grip on the sheet and took Callie's hand. "Thank you."

Ida snorted. "Callie, you're as tenderhearted as your cousin."

Callie laughed. "Don't be offended by my mama, Mrs. Davis. She sounds hard but she's not."

"She is being careful," Rachel said. "I would worry just as much if I were in her shoes." Ben noted Rachel's voice had a smoky, seductive quality. Raw silk.

Ida's frown eased. "Seems you're the only one with a bit of sense here." She studied Rachel closer this time. She approached and laid the back of her hand on Rachel's forehead. "My word, dear, you're hotter than a fritter. Are you feeling all right?"

Rachel nodded slowly as if the action required great effort. "I'm just tired."

Ben's annoyance drowned in concern as he moved to Rachel. "She was colder than ice last night."

Ida glanced over at her shoulder at Ben. "Ever consider extra blankets?"

"I tried that first," he said, teeth clenched.

Ida studied Rachel closely. "Ben is right. You need to stay in bed. Don't waste another bit of energy. We don't want the chill to settle in your lungs."

Rachel started to move toward the bed, but in two steps she crumbled. Ben scooped her up in his arms and laid her on the bed. He pulled the blankets up over her.

Relieved to withdraw to the comfort of her pillows and blankets, she eased back and closed her eyes. Her blond hair draped the white pillow. She looked drained. "I just need rest."

Ida laid the back of her hand on Rachel's forehead. "Aye, you are warm. Ben, how long was she in the water?"

"Thirty minutes after I found her, but before that I don't know."

"Hours," Rachel said. "I lost count."

"Ben, I don't like the look of her."

He'd battled too damn hard to save her to loose her to a fever. "I've Yaupon tea," he said.

Ida nodded. "Good idea. That'll help any fever. Brew it strong and keep her in bed. If she doesn't improve by morning, we'll send to the mainland for the doctor."

Rachel's eyes, bright with fear, widened. "No!

I'm sure a doctor isn't necessary. I just need a bit of rest."

Her reaction didn't surprise Ben. A woman on a freighter. A black eye. "The doctor's a good man, Rachel. There's no need to fear him. And he is discreet."

"I'm not afraid," she said, lifting her chin. "I will be fine. In fact, if I could just have my dress."

Ben wasn't convinced—not by a long shot.

And judging by the softening look on Ida's face, she wasn't convinced, either. With only the strength in his index finger, he pushed her back on the pillows. "Your dress is in a wet heap on the floor. And you're not moving a muscle."

Ignoring him, Rachel sat forward. "Perhaps, then, I could just trouble you ladies for a dress. I could trade mine for it. Once it is dry you will see that it is a fine dress."

"When you are well, I will happily see to getting you a dress. For now, listen to Ben, dear," Ida cautioned. "Your health could take a turn and you would find yourself in real trouble."

Clutching the blankets, Rachel boldly swung her legs over the side of the bed. She paused, clearly dizzy. Her mind wanted more than her body could manage.

The woman was stubborn, Ben thought.

She started to crumple forward.

Ben wrapped calloused hands on her bare shoulders. Her skin burned with the heat of a fever now. He eased her back against the pillows.

Rachel's breathing was ragged. "I really must leave."

She was weaker than a kitten and it took only a slight nudge to settle her.

"Lady, only a fool or a runaway would try to leave in your condition," Ben said evenly. "So tell me, which are you?"

Chapter Five

"I'm not a runaway," Rachel said, feeling the color drain from her face. She shrank back against the pillows. "I—I just don't want to be a bother."

"You're not a bother," Ida said brusquely.

Callie nodded her agreement. "We love to have visitors in town. We're fairly isolated out here."

Ben stood silent. His hair disheveled, dark stubble covering his square jaw. He looked like a pirate.

His sharp gaze cut into her, as if he were peeling away her protective layers and looking into her soul. This man was a hunter. He missed little.

She'd have to tread carefully. "I'm not used to being pampered," she said, trying to add strength to her words.

"Tough," he said. "Ida and Callie, see that she doesn't get out of that bed."

The women nodded. "She's not going anywhere until her cheeks aren't so flushed," Ida said.

"And that fever is gone," Callie said. "Yaupon tea and rest is what she needs."

"Callie, lets get to town and fetch more tea and herbs," Ida said. "We'll be back in a hour or so."

Rachel could have protested, but no one would have listened. And the truth was, they were right. She was too sick to travel.

Ben thanked his aunt and cousin and escorted them to the door. She listened to his steady purposeful steps echo in the house. Having him close made her feel safe.

When he returned, he went to the hearth. Squatting, he took the black iron and shoved it into the glowing logs. Sparks flicked up the chimney. He tossed a fresh log onto the flames.

His well-muscled shoulders strained against his woolen shirt. She'd had a taste of his power last night when he'd carried her in his arms. She'd been exhausted and had melted against him. She'd felt protected in his arms.

"Ida is worried you are trouble," he said.

Rachel moistened her lips. "I know."

"The *Anna St. Claire* is known for her rough crew. It's no place for a lady."

Tension tingled through her tired muscles. "As I said before, it was expedient."

Deliberately he replaced the iron and rose. He faced her. "Are you wanted by the law?"

Her heart slammed into her ribs. "No."

He studied her so intently, her cheeks, flushed with fever, paled a fraction. Lord, but her head was swimming.

"So if I telegrammed the sheriff in Elizabeth City, he'd not have heard of you?"

She sat up so fast, her stomach lurched and her sheet fell. Quickly she groped at its edges. The cool morning air had made her nipples harden into soft peaks. "Don't do that!"

Ben dropped his gaze while she righted her sheet. "Davis is your last name."

Was that the name she'd given last night? "Yes."

A humorless smiled curved the edges of his lips. "Davis. A solid American name."

Ordinary is what he meant to say. But that was why she must have chosen it. She wanted to blend in—to be one of a million faceless people that no one gave a second glance.

"Rachel Davis." The name sounded seductive, far from ordinary, when he spoke it.

Her head pounded and all she wanted to do was to lose herself in the blankets. "Yes."

"Where are you from?"

Hadn't he asked her that question last night? Details would be her downfall if she wasn't careful. With her senses so befuddled now, she'd never remember the lies she spun. "A small town. I doubt you've heard of it."

He raised an eyebrow. "Try me."

A gentleman would have taken her subtle hint and dropped the subject. "Do we really have to talk now? I'm so tired." Exhausted, her shoulders sagged.

He crossed to her in two steps and steadied her shoulders with his strong hands. Gently he guided her back to the pillows. "Aye, you do need your rest. But we will talk later."

She wasn't fooled by his kindness. Peter, too, could be kind. And kindness could be used as a lure into a snare.

He pulled the heavy blanket over her body. Despite the fever, the warmth of the blanket felt good.

"You're acting like a woman with a lot to hide, Rachel."

She moistened her dry lips. Why couldn't he leave her be? "I swear to you I'm not wanted by the authorities."

He tucked the blankets around her thin body. Gently he brushed the loose strands of hair off her forehead with calloused fingers.

His masculine scent enveloped her. For an instant, time stopped. She was aware only of him… and the beating of her heart. "No, I don't believe you are."

Rachel imagined that this was what a lover's touch must feel like. Tender. Soft. Gentle.

This man, she realized, was doubly dangerous.

Not only did questions lurk behind his gray eyes, but he had her dreaming of kindness and lover's touches—things she'd given up on soon after she'd married a monster. If only she'd never met Peter.

She met Ben's direct gaze. "Don't worry about me. I will be fine."

His eyes narrowed a fraction. Once again he was trying to peer into her soul.

Finally he withdrew. "If you're not wanted by the law, I guess that means you're a runaway. The question now is, who are you running from?"

Her skin itched with fear. "Stay out of my business, Mr. Mitchell."

Ben shoved his hands into his pockets. "I wish that I could." He rose and left the room.

Ben couldn't put Rachel out of his mind.

He spent the better part of the next half hour brewing Yaupon tea for her.

Rachel Davis had secrets.

He'd be wise to leave her to her demons. She wasn't his problem or his concern. And his days of taking on other people's battles were over.

Still, he'd been glad when the kettle had hissed and the dried leaves had turned the water to tea. Returning to her room with the tea was an excuse to see her. And he liked being close to her.

He carried the tin cup filled with tea to her room. The brew would help her fever and it would also give him another chance to talk to her.

However, to his disappointment, she'd fallen asleep. She lay curled on her side, her small hands fisted in front of her as if she would wake up fighting if he startled her awake.

Trouble. She was trouble.

He set the mug of tea down on chest beside the bed.

His gaze trailed over her full breasts, past the gentle curve of her hip and down her slender legs.

Aye, she had a siren's body.

But she was more than that. Intelligence lingered behind her blue eyes. And she possessed strength. It had taken guts to board a vessel like the *Anna St. Claire* and courage not to crumble when the freighter had started to sink.

Rachel mumbled something in her sleep and

rolled away from him. He saw her bruise. A fist had made that bruise. And the marks on her arms were clearly finger imprints.

Annoyed, he turned and walked to his dresser. From the second drawer, he pulled out a clean cable-knit sweater. The one from last night was still damp and smelled of seaweed.

He tugged the sweater over his head. Like everything else he owned, the black garment was practical—anything that wasn't functional had no place in his life.

As he smoothed the sweater over his flat belly, Rachel started to speak.

"I know what I need to do," she said.

"I've tea," he said, annoyed that his veins sang with anticipation.

"I know."

Adjusting the sleeves around his wrists, he turned. She still lay curled on her side, facing him. Her eyes were closed. She was talking in her sleep.

Her feet pushed and kicked under the sheet and blankets. Her face was knotted in a frown.

"Peter, no!" she wailed.

Ben moved to the bed and sat on the edge. He laid his hand on her shoulder. She started, as if defending herself. She swung her fist wildly, catching him squarely in the chest.

Recoiling, he inhaled a breath, biting back the jolt of pain and an oath. For a tiny woman, she packed one hell of a punch.

She was having a nightmare. "Rachel, wake up."

This time he grabbed her wrists. He noted she felt hotter than before, yet she still fought harder, kicking her legs like a hellcat.

Ben could feel her pulse in her wrist pounding furiously against his fingertips.

This was the kind of strength borne of fear.

"Rachel. It's all right. It's Ben. Peter isn't here."

Her thrashing slowed.

"Peter is not here," he repeated. "You are safe. Peter is gone."

She whimpered and stopped fighting. She relaxed back against her pillows. Slowly the frown lines creasing her brow eased.

Seeing her so distraught made him angry. What the devil had happened to her? Whoever the hell Peter was, he'd done one hell of a job of scaring Rachel.

When Rachel awoke, the sun outside was bright, slashing through the window into the room. Her fever had broken and her head no longer pounded. Immediately she sat up in her bed, wondering how long she'd been asleep. Her heart racing, she frantically searched the room for a clock.

How much time had she wasted? She had to get out of this place before Peter found her.

She scanned the room for something to wear. She spotted a large shirt draped over the edge of her bed. Her head swam as she leaned forward and with a trembling hand grabbed hold of the shirt. Pausing, she took several deep breaths until her body settled.

The shirt, no doubt that was Keeper Mitchell's doing. Though clean, his musky scent still clung to the coarse, blue fabric. She lifted the sleeve to her nose and inhaled deeply. Oddly, his shirt had a calming effect on her. She felt safe.

"There's no such thing as safe," she whispered.

She yanked the fabric over her head and fastened the four buttons. Slowly she swung her legs over the side of the bed. The cold floor bit into her bare feet.

The bed was still warm and it temped her. She'd have liked nothing more than to lie back and rest a few more hours.

But Peter would soon return home. She had to find her clothes and move on. To her disappointment, her clothes were gone. Then she remembered the older woman—Ida—she'd said she'd launder the clothes.

Relax. One step at a time.

There was little concession to luxury in Ben's room. As simple as a Spartan warrior's, the room was furnished with a large chest by the bed, an old dresser and a worktable and chair covered with charts and maps. The walls were a stark white. No pictures or curtains adorned the room.

Frustrated, she looked around the keeper's room for more clothing. She rose. Her legs wobbled. She held on to the bedpost and waited as her legs grew stronger. When she was certain she could walk, she moved to the dresser in search of pants. She opened the drawers and found pants in the third one down.

She held up the heavy cotton pants. They were Ben's and clearly too large for her. She'd not be able to keep them up.

Clothes. She needed clothes.

Where was Ben? He would help once he saw that she was better.

Ben's shirttail brushed against her bare thighs as she walked to the window. It was cracked open an inch. A steady sea breeze blew inside.

She inhaled deeply, savoring the fresh air and the unexpected warmth. The air here was so clean and unlike the city air, which always smelled of garbage in the streets and horse dung.

She squinted against the bright sunshine as she

stared over the sandy yard. To her right stood the lighthouse with its bold white and black stripe. It stood in sharp contrast to azure sky.

Rachel looked up the spiral to the light tower at the top. The light was extinguished now, but she'd remembered the night of her rescue. It had blinked so bright. She'd clung to it while she'd been on the *Anna St. Claire* staring out the portal, knowing it was her only link to the land.

Beyond the lighthouse stood the dunes. Tall sea oats swayed gently in the wind. There was a peace and serenity here that was so alluring. This was the kind of place she could call home. If not for Peter, she might have been tempted to stay awhile.

Peter. Her skin prickled. She wondered what he was doing now. Had he arrived in Washington? Did he know she'd left? Time was running out. She could feel it in her bones.

A light knock on the door had her starting and turning. She hurried to the bed, grabbed a blanket and draped it over her shoulders.

"Yes," she said.

"It's Keeper Mitchell. May I come in?"

Immediately she felt her shoulders relax even as her inside tightened. "Yes."

He pushed open the door with his foot. In his hand he carried a tray, which held a steaming bowl of broth and a mug filled with coffee. "It's good to see that you're up."

Memories of last night were jumbled at best. She remembered the keeper's strong embrace and his soothing voice, but she'd not remembered what a truly attractive man he was.

His face looked chiseled from granite. His rich, black hair was dark as Satan's and hung past his collar. This morning he'd brushed it back and tied it with a strip of rope. His clear gray eyes made her skin tingle each time he looked her.

Rachel was suddenly aware that her waist-length hair was in a terrible tangle. She must look like one of those wild Amazonian women from the old fables. If only she could muster the strength of a warrior woman. She felt frightened and scared. "I only just woke up. I've slept the morning away."

He set the tray on the table. "More like the day and the next night away. It's Thursday morning."

A wave of panic washed over Rachel. "Thursday!" Already her head was spinning. Dear Lord, Peter had returned to Washington. "You should have woken me up."

"You needed the sleep."

Fists clenched at her sides, she started to pace. "You should have woken me."

Ben lifted an eyebrow. "Why is this a problem? Do you have to be somewhere?"

She needed to run! To be as far from Washington as she could get.

But Rachel didn't say that. She kept her feelings hidden—another talent Peter had taught her. Fear, anger, happiness could be used against her.

Inwardly, she was a mess, but she managed to calm the rigid muscles in her back and smile. "No, it's just that I have friends waiting for me. I don't want them to worry."

Ben stared at her. "There's a telegraph office on the mainland. When Timothy goes for supplies in a day or two, I could ask him to send a telegram."

"That won't be necessary. As soon as I get to the mainland, I can take care of it myself. I don't—"

He held up his hand, interrupting her. "I know. You don't want to cause me any more trouble."

She heard the sarcasm in his voice. "Why is that so hard for you to believe?"

He studied her a long moment, then shook his head. To her surprise he said, "Save your stories and eat your broth. It's going to get cold, and Ida and Callie were adamant that it be warm when you ate it."

Grateful for the reprieve, she dropped her gaze to the broth. She hated lying to him, but survival outweighed feelings.

She moved to the table and sat down. The rich smell of the beef broth teased her nose. Her stomach grumbled, signaling that she was hungrier than she realized. She took a taste. It was delicious.

Aware that his dark gaze hadn't left her, she felt compelled to make conversation. "Ida has outdone herself, Mr. Mitchell," she said.

He shrugged, but there was pride in his eyes. "She's one of the best cooks on the outer banks."

"I've no doubt she is." She'd not intended to eat the entire bowl but before she realized it the broth was gone.

"There's more if you want it," he said.

Her stomach rumbled. Peter had strictly regulated what she ate. Though she could eat as much as she wanted now, she had trouble allowing herself more. "No, I'm fine."

Ben muttered an oath. "You're half starved, yet you won't eat more." Without another word, he snatched up her empty bowl and strode out of the room. His purposeful steps echoed in the house.

Rachel rose, unsure of what she'd done to make him so angry. Fear knotted her stomach, yet she faced the door and waited for his return. She'd promised herself after she'd fled her home four days ago that she'd not cower anymore. She fisted her trembling fingers.

He reappeared minutes later with another bowl of soup and set it on the table. "Sit and eat. You're nothing but skin and bones."

She glanced down at her frame. When she'd first been introduced into society many had admired her looks, calling her attractive, beautiful even. So to be called "skin and bones" piqued at her pride. "I'm not *that* thin."

He took her by the elbow and guided her to the table. He gently pushed her into the chair. "I've seen five-year-old children who weigh more."

More irritated, she picked up her spoon. "So you're saying I look like a child?"

His glaze flickered to her breasts. "I didn't say that."

His voice had turned unexpectedly smoky. The last thing she needed was for any man to take notice of her now. She needed to blend in, to disappear.

But the fact that Ben liked the shape of her body pleased her.

Her appetite growing, she finished the second bowl under the keeper's watchful eye. Her stomach full now, she felt an odd sense of contentment. In fact, she felt more energized than she had in a year. "Thank you. I feel wonderful."

He grunted, satisfied. "The scavengers are out on the *Anna St. Claire* today. I can have them keep an eye out for any trunks you might have had aboard."

Of course, it would add fuel to his suspicions if she confessed she had no luggage. "My trunks were belowdecks," she lied. "I doubt they will find them."

"Likely not," he said.

Again he stared at her as if he were trying to read her mind. But he shrugged off whatever thoughts plagued him. "After you've eaten, I can take you to the village. Ida cleaned your dress."

"Wonderful." Her first lucky break. Absently, Rachel rubbed her ring finger, where her wedding band had been. In her mind, she'd never felt married. There'd been no love, yet she had tried until his fists had shattered any commitment she'd made to him.

"With luck, you can be out of here on tomorrow's boat to the mainland."

"Excellent."

For the first time in days she felt as if the fates were finally smiling on her.

Peter Emmons stepped from the carriage onto the sidewalk in front of his Washington town house. He inhaled, savoring the sweet smells of the city. Rachel wasn't outside waiting for him. He didn't like her outside of the house. She was learning.

He strode up the main steps and into the foyer. He inspected everything, pleased that nothing had changed since he'd left. He'd trained Rachel well. She understood that this was his house and nothing changed without his approval.

Ah, his sweet Rachel. He'd missed her. Three days was a long time. Time enough for her to pick up bad habits. She always was too willful for his tastes.

Strong discipline kept her line. And under his guidance, she was slowly becoming the perfect wife. So much work, but it had been worth it.

Peter looked forward to assessing Rachel—how much retraining would need to be done.

Impatient to see his wife, he climbed the stairs two at a time and pushed through the front door. To his shock, she wasn't there waiting for him. "Rachel!"

The grandfather clock in the hallway ticked slowly. "Rachel!" The woman had forgotten to jump when she heard his voice.

Footsteps sounded on the upstairs landing. He glanced up, expecting to see his sweet Rachel. He'd have to teach her about tardiness.

To his great disappointment, the maid appeared. He could never remember the twit's name.

"Where is Mrs. Emmons?" he shouted.

The maid cringed and took a step back.

Simpering fool. "Where is she?"

Her face paled a fraction until it was nearly the color of her very starched apron. "She's gone, sir."

"What do you mean, *gone?*"

She swallowed, lifting her gaze. "Three days ago, she left for the market. She said she was going to pick a gift out for your anniversary. We expected her to be gone no more than an hour. But she never came back."

Rage boiled his veins. "What!"

Tears flooded down the woman's face. She curtsied. "We've searched everywhere, sir. The police, the hospitals, the train stations. She's not anywhere to be found."

How dare she.

The maid added quickly, "The butler has had runners at the docks and inns searching discreetly for her. She's vanished without a trace."

"Everyone leaves clues," he said, jerking off his gloves.

And he'd find the ones Rachel had left.

He remembered the way she'd spoken to that man at the party last week. The bitch had likely run off with a lover.

He would do whatever it took to find his wife. And when he did, Rachel was going to pay.

Chapter Six

Later that afternoon Rachel put on Timothy's baggy clothes. She rolled the pant cuffs up four times, shoved back the black cotton shirtsleeves and cinched the waistband with a length of rope.

Timothy was a head shorter than Ben, and still the clothes swallowed her. Her black eye had all but faded but she still looked as rough as the sailors she'd seen on the docks. No matter how many times she fussed with the shirt and pants, there seemed no way to make herself look presentable.

She ran her fingers through her waist-length hair, trying her best to work out the knots. Without a comb, the task was impossible. In the end, she settled for a loose braid tied with a strand of twine.

She felt self-conscious. Since she'd been in the nursery, she'd always been expected to present herself as a well-dressed lady. Peter had been particularly adamant that she dress well at all times. Logically she understood that she was enduring extenuating circumstances. Runaway, shipwrecked with no clothes to her name, it was a miracle she'd survived. She should be grateful for what she had. But years of conditioning had her worrying about breaches of etiquette. Peter would be furious if he saw her.

Fear gathered tight in her throat. Breaking the rules had always meant consequences. Peter had seen to that. Rachel unrolled her right sleeve.

Rachel stopped. "No, I won't play that game anymore. I am free of him."

"Rachel," Ben called from the hallway. "Lunch is getting cold. Come now or I'll feed your food to the dogs."

Annoyed, she glanced at the closed door. "I'm coming."

"That's what you said five minutes ago."

She gave her anger and frustration full rein. "I'm hurrying!"

"Lord help us if you take your time."

Exasperated, she quickly folded her sleeve back up. "Just another minute."

"I'm coming in."

He was bluffing.

The door opened. Ben stood on the threshold, his broad shoulders blocking her view of the hallway. "No more minutes. You need to eat."

Despite her best intention, she hesitated. "But I'm not presentable."

His gaze trailed up her body, lingering on her full breasts that not even her baggy clothes could hide. "You look good to me."

His deep male tone had her blushing. "I look like a boy."

"Not even close." He took a step back, as if he needed distance. "You are a woman in need of clothes, which is why we're headed to town after we eat. The sooner you get your fanny out of this room and eat, the sooner you'll have a dress."

He was right, of course. She was being unreasonable. "I just ate broth an hour ago."

"Doesn't count." He turned and, taking her arm, started toward the kitchen.

"I'm not hungry."

"Humor me."

She followed him down the hallway. The kitchen was simple, furnished only with a large table and six chairs around it. On the west wall stood a cast-iron stove. Above it hung shelves filled with neatly arranged canned goods and tins. A fine coating of dust covered everything, and there wasn't a curtain or a carpet to warm the wide-paneled pine floor.

A man's domain, she thought. Simple and practical.

The smell of eggs and bacon filled the room and to her surprise her stomach rumbled.

"Sit," he said.

Having a man wait on her felt awkward. There'd been servants in her home but when one wasn't available it was understood that she fetched the coffee, muffins or whatever needed getting. Her father and Peter had never waited on her once.

She stood next to the chair. "Can I help with anything?"

"Sit." He filled a white plate with a hefty portion of eggs and bacon. "Do you drink coffee?"

Tea was more her to her tastes, but she'd never have said so. Then again she stopped herself. She wasn't going to be afraid to ask anymore. "Do you have tea?"

To her surprise he nodded. "Coming right up."

Minutes later he set a basket of muffins and then a plate of eggs and bacon in front of her along with a mug of tea. The food smelled delicious. She took a bite. It tasted even better. "I've never known a man to cook."

He shrugged as he ladled more food onto another plate. "The muffins are Ida's. As to the rest, if a man out here wants to eat, he learns to cook."

"Most of the men I know have servants to wait on them."

He grinned. His entire face softened and he looked doubly handsome. He set a plate of eggs down at his place.

"I'm not like the men you're used to."

An unfamiliar sensation warmed her body. Ben Mitchell was nothing like the city men with their silk vests and uncalloused hands. The keeper possessed an earthy masculinity that made her very aware she was a woman.

"No, I suppose you're not."

He sat at his own plate. "Eat."

She started to eat and was pleasantly surprised to discover the food was good. "Where'd you learn to cook?"

"Ida mostly. She and my uncle raised me after my folks died."

She was very curious about him. "I've not met your uncle."

"He died five years ago. His heart failed."

Ben's somber tone spoke to his sadness. Her father had been dead just over a year. However, there wasn't any great sadness, only a lingering regret that they'd never been close.

For a moment she didn't speak. "So you've lived here all your life, Mr. Mitchell?"

"Barring my years in the Navy, yes." A lock of hair swept down over his forehead. "We spent a night together naked and in each other arms, Rachel. I think you can call me Ben."

A wave of heat washed over her and it had nothing to do with the fever she'd had. He possessed a seductive, rugged quality that made her knees weak. "I don't think that's proper."

He grinned, leaning toward her. "Rachel, you left proper behind when you boarded the *Anna St. Claire.*"

He was right. She'd left everything behind the day she'd boarded that ship. "All right, B-Ben."

Ben glanced up toward the ceiling. "Doesn't look like there's a bolt of lightening headed your way."

She followed his gaze. "I don't understand."

Laughter danced in his eyes. "I'll bet your nursemaids and teachers told you the heavens would strike you down if you broke the rules of etiquette."

She couldn't resist a smile. "Actually, there were gremlins in the night that took care of naughty girls."

He lifted an eyebrow. "Seriously?"

"Quite. Mrs. Wentworth, she ran my boarding school, went into great detail about the monsters waiting for bad little girls."

The humor vanished from his eyes. "That's awful."

"And effective." She'd not thought of Mrs. Wentworth in years. "We called her Mama Hippo behind her back."

He grinned. "Good for you."

She felt herself relaxing. She sipped her tea. "How long were you in the Navy?"

"Twelve years."

Rachel broke off a bite-size piece of crisp bacon. "And you just quit and came back here?"

Tension tightened his shoulders. "I had good reasons."

"I didn't mean to pry, Mr. Mitchell."

"Ben."

The back door banked open and Timothy walked in. Rachel sat straighter, her defenses up again. He shrugged off his coat. "You're up," he said to Rachel. "Good to see it. Thought we were going to lose you there at first."

Rachel glanced at Ben. He frowned at the boy. "I remember being cold."

"Cold," Timothy said. "Lady, you were blue."

"Boy, make yourself a plate and eat," Ben said. "Rachel doesn't need to hear any of that."

Timothy scooped eggs and bacon from the cast iron pan onto a white earthenware plate. He took his place at the table. "Sorry, ma'am. I didn't mean to scare you."

"It's no wonder I was blue," she said. "The ocean was like ice." She took another bite.

Ben picked up one of Ida's muffins. "Much going on in town?"

Timothy shrugged as he took two large bites of food. "Callie wants to see Rachel again. She's real curious about her. Ida doesn't say too much about Rachel, but she always listens when her name's brought up."

Rachel glanced up. It wasn't good to be noticed. "Why?"

"You're a miracle lady. Everyone up and down the banks is talking about you."

Rachel set her fork down. First the sailors had thought her cursed. Now the villagers saw her as a miracle. She couldn't have been more obvious if she'd tried. She barely heard much else for the next few minutes.

Timothy took a sip of coffee. "Ben, the seas are calm enough today so I'll head to the mainland at first light for supplies. I can also send a telegram to the shipping company."

"Good." Ben glanced at her as if he sensed the change in her mood.

Rachel felt a prickle of alarm. "Telegram?"

"About the *Anna St. Claire,*" Ben explained. "We always telegram the company to let them know what we've found."

Including her. Word of her on the freighter would spread like wildfire. Peter would find her in no time.

"You've not sent the telegram?"

"Not yet," Timothy said.

There was still time. The tension in her voice slid over Timothy's head. But not Ben's.

"If you don't mind, I'm going to take a walk outside."

Ben stared at her over the rim of his cup. "We can go into town now if you like."

"No, no, please finish your lunch." Dear Lord, she had to get out of here. She'd all but left a trail of bread crumbs for Peter to follow.

She went outside. Her chest tight, she could barely breathe.

The sky was blue and the air fresh. It was a spectacular day. But fear tainted the colors and scents.

The back door opened and closed. Ben strode out. He'd pulled on a dark jacket and in his hand carried a spare. "You need a coat."

Automatically she slid her hands into the coat. More oversize than the shirt or pants, Rachel realized that this coat didn't belong to Timothy but Ben.

His scent was burned into the coarse fabric, enveloping her as if his arms were wrapped around her.

"Your name will be omitted from the telegram," Ben said.

Relief wash over her, but a lingering tightness in her stomach left her sick. "Thank you."

"Ready to go into town?" he said, his lips close to her ear.

Rachel nodded. "Yes. Is it far to town?"

He took her by the elbow. "A half mile."

They walked across the lawn toward a sandy path that cut through a grove of wind-stunted pines. Ben slid glances her way. She sensed his questions, yet he didn't say anything. Just a matter of time, she thought. He wasn't the kind of man to ignore conflict.

A heavy silence hung between them as the breeze flapped the loose folds of her shirt. She smelled the tang of the salt air. Bright sunshine warmed her face.

She inhaled deeply, trying to soften the tension between them. "It feels like we are a million miles away from anywhere."

He nodded. "When the weather closes in, we might as well be."

A strand of hair came loose from her braid. She tucked it behind her ear. "Is the weather bad here a lot?"

"Often enough."

The sound of the ocean, the squawk of gulls and the breeze acted like a tonic. "There is magic in this place. It almost reminds me of Camelot, the enchanted kingdom that vanished into the mists."

The creases around his eyes deepened as he smiled. "On days like today, it is magic. But this land can turn fierce."

"Isn't that the way it always is? Life gives with one hand and takes with the other. Even the rose has thorns."

He studied her. "Cynical for one so young."

"Once upon a time I was quite the romantic. I dreamed of fairy-tale endings and white knights."

"But no more," he said gently.

The urge to let her guard down was powerful. Whether it was this place, Ben or the loneliness, she couldn't say. She was so tempted to share her story and share her burden with someone else, but she couldn't succumb.

Rachel had learned to smile when times were the most tense. A smile had the power to deflect an unwanted question. "You must have seen many places when you were in the Navy."

Ben hesitated. He recognized the ploy. "Aye, I saw a good many ports."

"What was your favorite?"

"For a woman short on answers, you do have a good many questions."

His rebuke caught her up short. "Most gentlemen would honor a lady's desire to change the topic of conversation."

Ben shrugged. "Did I ever say I was a gentleman?"

In truth, with his black hair, hardened features and powerful build, he again reminded her of a buccaneer. "No, you did not."

"Going forward, if you want to ask a question, I'll answer it…provided you answer one of my questions to you."

She went silent.

"I thought that would shut you up." He took her elbow in his hand. She flinched, like a cat ready to spring.

Ben released his hold immediately. Pausing, he allowed her to move down the path ahead of him. "You are a puzzle, Rachel Davis."

With effort, she kept her voice even. But she was angry now, not with him but herself. She was tired of being scared and measuring every word. "Not really. In fact, I'm somewhat of a cliché. Very ordinary, very forgettable."

"Rachel, you are anything but ordinary and quite unforgettable."

She didn't want to be remembered. "You will forget me soon enough," she said.

"Doubtful."

It was a man's nature to notice a woman.

There were many pretty lasses on the outer banks, but Ben had seen none like Rachel. He appreciated the way a simple rope hugged her narrow waist; the way her long braid brushed the top of her backside; the way her chin lifted when she asked a question.

This gal had been born to money and it dripped out every pore of her body. She might have been wearing Timothy's spare clothes, but she bore herself as if she wore the finest ball gown.

But her prim-and-proper ways hadn't turned her into a cold woman. He'd seen the fire and curiosity spark in her eyes.

He glanced down at her ring finger, remembering she'd said she was a widow. For reasons he couldn't explain, it bothered him that she had belonged to another man.

He watched as she moved down the narrow path that cut through the center of the island and snaked toward the Sound side of the island and the tiny fishing village.

Soon she'd be gone from his life.

Neither spoke the remainder of the walk. When they emerged from the thicket, they followed a wide cart path several hundred yards before rounding a bend and seeing the village.

"The village isn't like the city," he said. "The village's weather-beaten buildings likely will look humble to you," he said. Many a survivor from a shipping accident had complained of the simple village and its lack of conveniences.

Rachel stopped and, shielding her eyes from the sun, studied the collection of buildings. "On the contrary, they are quite charming."

He studied her, searching for signs of insincerity. But there were none.

On the north end of town stood the general store run by Ida. Next to it stood Mae Talbert's pub. She ran a clean place and had six rooms—none were fancy but all were spit-'n'-polish clean. Down the main dirt street stood a small white church with its new wooden spire added only last fall.

Behind the building was the Sound. Piers jutted out from the sandy coastline into the waters. Today only a couple of boats bobbed from tethers tied to the docks. Most of the fisherman had left at dawn, ready to make up for the days lost during the last storm. It was the middle of the week so the children had been sent to board on the mainland for school. None of the residents liked giving up their children, but any who wanted an education for their young ones had no choice.

The main street was quiet, but the few women who spotted them stopped and openly stared at Rachel. No doubt, Ida and Callie had told the town about her. Most shipwreck survivors were men, sailors and fisherman and the few women generally traveled with their husbands or family. The fact that Rachel had been alone and traveling on a freighter made her an oddity.

"Hello there, Ben," called an older woman. Sara Crocket had just celebrated her eightieth year. She had been a young girl when the first lighthouse had been built on the island. She'd seen the tower partly destroyed in the '49 storm and witnessed the current lighthouse's construction ten years ago.

"Afternoon," he said to Mrs. Crocket.

Rachel fussed with her hair, pulling wisps loose to cover her bruised eye.

"It barely shows," he said.

Her gaze darted up to his. They were full of worry and shame.

If he could find the person who'd given her the bruise he'd have beaten him to a pulp. "Truly, it's almost faded."

Rachel stood a little straighter. "Thank you."

Mrs. Crocket crossed the street, hobbling. The damp weather always made her hip ache.

Ben took Rachel's arm. This time she didn't flinch. Pleased, he guided her toward Mrs. Crocket to save the old woman a step. They met in the center of the quiet street. "Hear you caught yourself a mermaid," she said, laughing. The sun had etched deep lines into her old narrow face and her thinning gray hair, always pulled back in a bun, had been silver for as long as he could remember.

"Not a mermaid," he said easily. "Just a woman with the bad fortune to be sailing these waters in a storm. Mrs. Crocket, meet Rachel Davis."

Mrs. Crocket studied Rachel, openly curious. "Davis, did you say? I don't know any Davis in these parts but there is a Lyle Davis in Elizabeth City. Are you kin to him?"

He sensed Rachel's reserve. "No, ma'am."

"Where you hail from, girl?"

"North."

"North!" Mrs. Crocket shook her head, her disgust clear. "Not too far *north* I hope. Folks ain't so fond of the Yanks around here." She winked at Ben. "Some folks still haven't forgiven Ben for siding with the Federals, and he grew up here."

Ben shrugged. He'd followed his conscious. The opinions of others didn't matter.

Right now, Rachel held his interest.

He noted the way her smile reached her eyes as she looked at the old woman. "No, ma'am, not too far north." She glanced into the woman's basket. "Is that bread I smell? It smells divine. Did you bake it?"

The older woman grinned at the compliment. She was unaware that Rachel had changed the course of the conversation. Rachel had a knack for deflecting questions.

North. It could mean Virginia or Canada, for all he knew. As the two women chatted about recipes, he wondered again where Rachel was from. The more she hid her past, the more compelled he was to find out more about it.

In a few short minutes Rachel had won over the older woman, who'd promised to bake her a loaf of bread tomorrow.

When they reached Ida's store, he had to smile. "You've a way with people."

She looked up at him, confused. "What do you mean?"

"I'd say you were genuinely interested in Mrs. Crocket's cooking,"

She frowned. "I was."

"You've never seen the inside of a kitchen, I'll wager."

"No, but I've read a few cookbooks. Some are so precise with their measurements, but she's never measured anything in her life. Uses just her senses when she cooks. That's very interesting to me."

"You read a lot."

"Not much lately."

"Why not?"

"Lots of reasons."

He climbed the front steps to Ida's mercantile and opened the door. Bells above the door jingled. "A beautiful woman like you reads, but doesn't live her life."

She stepped inside, ducking her head as she moved past him. "Books are a great escape."

"From what?"

Rachel arched an eyebrow. "You are so full of questions."

"Toss me one answer and I'll stop."

"So are we trading questions for questions now?"

He shrugged. "That was my offer."

Her eyes sparked with curiosity. "Why did you leave the Navy?"

He'd heard that very same question dozens of times. Other than Ida and Callie, he'd never answered it.

She lifted an eyebrow. "Ah, you don't want to

answer the question. You see? We all have subjects we don't want to talk about."

"All right," Ben said. "But then you owe me an answer to a question."

He was calling her bluff.

She took a step back. "You don't have to tell me anything. I—I shouldn't have pried."

He lifted a shoulder. "A deal's a deal." And before she could silence him, he said, "I was court-martialed."

Chapter Seven

Stunned, Rachel blinked, not sure what to say. Ben Mitchell seemed like the last man on this earth that the Navy would court-martial. He was solid and strong; a man who lived by a code of honor regardless of the dangers. He'd proved as much to her when he'd boarded the *Anna St. Claire* to rescue her. "Why would they court-martial you?"

Even white teeth flashed when he smiled. "Ah, that is another question. You owe me an answer now. Who hit you, Rachel?"

Before she could respond, Ida came out of the back room. "Are you two going to stand out in the wind all day or are you going to come inside where it's warm?"

"In just a minute, Ida," Ben said, his gaze

never wavering from Rachel's. "Rachel owes me an answer."

Ida sensed she'd intruded, retreated back into the shop and closed the door. However, Rachel could see that she hovered close, frowning, her arms folded over her chest.

"We can't keep Ida waiting," Rachel said. She didn't want Ida overhearing their conversation. The woman suspected she had secrets as it was.

"Watch me."

Ben's persistence didn't surprise her. She loathed answering any questions about a past she only wanted to forget, but her own curiosity about Ben had started this game. "Peter hit me."

His gaze narrowed. "Peter who?"

Like him, she'd given an honest answer that didn't begin to satisfy. "I've answered your question. We are even."

Frustration sparked in his eyes. "Who the devil is Peter?"

Her own curiosity about Ben had gotten her into this corner. She'd not be so foolish again. "No more questions and no more answers. I am done with this game."

He grabbed her arm. "It's no game. Was Peter your husband?"

She jerked away from him. "My husband is

dead!" She opened the shop door and slammed it closed behind her.

Ben was a smart man. In just days he'd touched painfully close to the truth. If she weren't careful, he'd discover everything.

Ida stood behind the store counter, her hands planted on her hips, her expression stern. "You two have an argument?"

Rachel moved toward the counter, grateful to have a little distance from Ben. "No, no, we were just talking."

Ben opened and closed the door. He stood with his back to the door, his arms folded over his chest. She could feel the energy radiating from him.

Ida's gaze traveled between the two of them. Her lips flattened as she took in Ben's dark gaze and Rachel's flushed cheeks. "Everything all right?"

"It's fine, Ida," Ben said. "Just fine." He moved down the center isle.

Ida lifted a brow. Clearly she didn't believe him but she seemed to sense this wasn't the time to push. "Rachel, you look better. Your coloring looks good," Ida said. "Ben must be taking good care of you."

She could feel him standing behind her, but she didn't dare turn around to look at him. "He's been kind."

"You drink plenty of Yaupon tea?"

Rachel managed a faltering smile. "I think I've drank enough of that tea to fill a lake."

Ida's gaze narrowed. "Your bruise is almost gone."

Self-conscious, Rachel raised her hand to her eye. She prayed once the bruise was gone, the questions would stop. She didn't want anyone to know what a miserable failure her life had become. "Yes, it's almost gone."

Ida's expression softened a fraction. A silent understanding passed between the women.

"You've nothing to be ashamed of, Rachel. Remember that."

Rachel straightened her shoulders. "I know."

Ben stood to Rachel's right. His arms crossed, he leaned against the counter. He absorbed every detail.

The front bells of the store jingled and Callie breezed inside. Her face was flushed from the chilly weather. She whisked a black scarf from her head and pulled off her brown overcoat.

"Rachel! I heard you were in town. I'm so glad you came. I went to see you yesterday, but Ben said you were sleeping. He was quite a pit bull— very protective."

"Seems I slept quite a long time."

Callie hung her coat and scarf on a peg. "No

wonder. I was on the beach this morning with Timothy and we were looking at the wreck. To think you were trapped inside." She shuddered. "Awful. I doubt that I could have been so brave."

"I am not so brave."

Callie smoothed back a loose strand of black hair. Her eyes shone with youthful appreciation. "Ah, but you are. Bruised and battered as you were and to keep your wits about you in a half-sunken ship—that is so very brave."

Ida cleared her throat. "Have you come for your dress?"

"Yes," Rachel said.

Callie laughed. "We can't have you running around the island in Timothy's clothes. We may be rural out this way but we do have some standards."

Rachel smoothed her hands over the rough wool pants. She felt all the more awkward in the young lightkeeper's clothes.

Ida cleared her throat at her daughter's boldness.

However, Callie didn't seem to notice. She moved toward a collection of dresses hung on a rack to the left of the counter. "We have some lovely dresses in," Callie said.

"I just need *my* dress," Rachel said.

Ida nodded. "I'll get it." She disappeared through the curtained door behind the counter.

Callie held up a deep blue sapphire dress. The fabric caught the sunlight just right. It had a high collar and white piping on the bodice and cuffs. She held it up in front of Rachel. "Ben, see how the color complements her eyes?"

His gaze pinned Rachel. "Aye, it suits her just fine."

"This dress was salvaged off a Spanish frigate this past winter. It looks a bit large for you, but that can easily be fixed. Cecilia Wharton is an excellent seamstress and she can have the dress altered in a week." Her face lit up. "She's making my wedding dress. I just had my last fitting this morning. Can you believe it? Timothy and I will be married in a couple of days!"

Rachel stared into the young girl's eyes so full of hope and excitement. Once she'd looked like that. "Good wishes to you both."

Callie draped the dress over the counter. The dress was lovely. Oh, to be rid of the black.

For an instant Rachel was drawn in by Callie's excitement. Without realizing it, she crossed the room and touched the fabric. It was beautiful. And very, very tempting. "It's lovely."

Callie grinned. "You should always wear bright colors, Rachel. You're too young to wear black."

"She's in mourning," Ben said.

Rachel dropped the fabric. The momentary excitement vanished. He was watching her closely. "Ben's right. It wouldn't be proper for me to wear the blue."

And the black was a perfect reminder of the mistakes she'd vowed never to make again.

"But you deserve something lovely," Callie persisted.

Rachel smiled at the young girl. "Even if I could wear the dress, my money is in my reticule at the bottom of the sea with the *Anna St. Claire.* I cannot afford the material."

Rachel felt no shame. Poverty was a small price to pay for her freedom.

Ida reappeared with Rachel's dress. The wool dress had been cleaned and pressed and looked almost as good as new. And it was very black and very austere, just as Callie had said.

"Black may be proper," Callie said, "but it doesn't suit you at all. It'll wash your fair complexion right out."

A year ago Rachel would have worried about her complexion. Now she was grateful just to have a warm, practical dress. "I'll survive."

"The woman knows what she wants," Ida said. "Stop pushing her, Callie."

"But, Mama, the dress costs us nothing. And no one around here is showing any interest in it. It's a shame to let it go to waste."

"Callie," Rachel said. "No."

"You should try it on," Ben said.

Color rose in Rachel's face. She'd made her decision and didn't appreciate Ben's interfering. "I thank you all for your kindness, but there's no point. I can't wear the dress now, and even if I could, I can't afford it."

"I will pay for it," Ben said.

Rachel shook her head. Ben wasn't just offering her the dress. He was challenging her story. He suspected she wasn't in mourning. "No."

"How long to alter the dress?" Ben said to Callie. Ida groaned.

Callie's eyes lit up. "If I nudge the seamstress, a couple of days."

Rachel's heart hammered in her chest. Ben was backing her into a corner. "I don't have the time. I really must be leaving the peninsula as soon as is possible."

Ida nodded. "Sloan operates a ferry. He's left for today but he'll make a run tomorrow. You can leave at daybreak."

The news didn't excite Rachel as she'd thought it would. "Good."

Ben kept his feelings hidden. "What would it hurt to try the dress on?"

Rachel could forgive Callie's enthusiasm. She was young. Ben's motives were calculated. He challenged her story. "Accepting a gift from a man, *Mr. Mitchell,* suggests an understanding between them. There could be no understanding between us."

In her mind and heart, her union with Peter was dissolved, but legally she would be shackled to him until death parted them.

"When you come out of mourning, you will need clothes."

Rachel prayed for patience. "My dress is all that *I* need."

Ben didn't miss her meaning.

"Try it on," Callie urged.

"I can't." Rachel handed the dress back to Ida. *"I can't."* Her frustration had quickly soured to anger.

Respect sparked in Ida's eyes.

"Wrap it up," Ben said, his tone softening. "And whatever frippery goes with it, Ida."

"Mama has the loveliest chemise," Callie said.

"Callie, I'll let you take care of the details," Ben said.

The fact that Ben and Callie discussed her intimate apparel didn't even faze Rachel. She was too angry to care. "You two aren't listening to me. I won't accept it."

Callie hummed as she collected all manner of stockings, bows, shoes and stockings. "Well, then, Ben is going to look mighty silly decked out in this dress. Blue is not his color."

The humor was lost on Rachel. Callie and Ben were backing her into a corner and she didn't like it.

"Listen, to me!" Rachel said.

"I think you'd wear our smallest lady's undergarments."

"I don't want the dress or anything else! My money is at the bottom of the ocean and I won't take charity."

Callie and Ben stared at her, surprise etched on their faces. Ida smiled approvingly.

"I won't be invisible any longer or let others make the decisions in my life!" Rachel scooped up her black dress and ran outside. Tears of frustration burned her eyes.

She hurried down the boardwalk and toward a narrow path unsure of where she was going. Soon she reached a small beach that ringed the Sound. A collection of piers jutted into the smooth waters. She stopped.

Her stomach tumbled at the sight of the Sound. Lord, but she hated the water.

She walked along the narrow beach until she reached an overturned dinghy. She sat on the edge of the boat, the black dress balled in her lap. Tears pooled in her eyes as she stared out over the glassy water.

She laid her head in her lap. The thick black wool itched her skin.

Her life was a mess.

She'd behaved like a lunatic. Callie was only trying to help. Yet she'd balked like a caged animal and run screaming from the store. No doubt they'd be quite happy to be rid of her now.

And Ben was too perceptive. It was a matter of time before he figured out her secrets.

She wasn't sure how long she sat there, but she was aware the instant Ben came up beside her. His shadow blocked the sun from her face.

"I'm sorry," he said. "I shouldn't have pushed the dress."

She looked up. The sun shone behind him, accentuating his broad shoulders. Peter had never apologized to her. Neither had her father. In fact, she didn't know men did such things.

The power of "I'm sorry" amazed her. The words washed away her anger instantly. "You and Callie were only trying to help."

He sat beside her on the edge of the boat. He

clasped his calloused hands in front of him. "I was pushy and overbearing. I suppose an overbearing attitude is a holdover from the Navy. I'm used to giving commands and having them obeyed." His shoulder brushed against hers. "You were very clear about what you wanted. I just wasn't listening. Ida gave Callie and I quite a lecture."

A tear trickled down her cheek. She wiped it away. "I'm normally not so ungrateful. There was a time when I was a happy woman."

He lifted the hem of the black dress. Absently he rubbed it between his fingers. "Tell me about Peter." No command this time.

His question caught her off guard. She wiped another tear from her cheek and faced him. "I don't want to play this game anymore."

"I'm not playing." He took her left hand in his, absently rubbing her ring finger. The indent left by her wedding ring had vanished. "Tell me why you are running."

Wind whipped her hair as she stared into his steady gaze. Power, strength and gentleness radiated from him. He'd been so good to her. And she sensed he was a decent man. He'd keep her secret. But it was a burden he didn't deserve.

"No," she said.

He frowned.

"You can trust me, Rachel," he said softly. "Talk to me. Tell me what is bothering you, who you are afraid of. I can help."

Oh, Lord, but she wanted to tell him everything. "Ben, there are some problems no amount of talking or wishing can fix."

Ben stared at her a long moment, his face full of questions. He clearly didn't like it when he couldn't control a situation.

Finally he dragged in a deep breath, releasing it slowly as if he'd come to a decision. "The living is hard here, and we don't have many fancy things, but the water and the ocean are natural barriers to the outside world. If you're looking for a place to start over or hide, Rachel, this place is it."

A place to start over.

The words tumbled in Rachel's head. "I need to keep moving."

"You're a beautiful woman. You will stick out when you arrive on the mainland. I've no doubt the sailors on the *Anna St. Claire* took note of you."

She remembered the lean, hungry gazes of the sailors. "I've been noticed here."

"Aye, but we are a close-knit group here. No one will say a word about you if I ask it."

So tempting.

Sunshine glinted on the crests of the rippling

waters. The crests sparkled. A fish jumped out of the water.

Ben laced his fingers between hers. "I can understand if you don't want to tell me about your past for now. I was there once myself. But you can't keep running. It's not safe."

He offered a truce. He was willing to let the past be forgotten. *A place to start over.* "I don't know if I have the courage to stop running. I've turned into a coward."

He raised their interlocked hands to his chest. "You are not a coward."

Tears burned her throat. Rachel shielded her eyes and stared toward the mainland over the Sound's waters. It seemed so far away.

Rachel's racing heart slowed. She leaned her shoulder against his. He made her feel safe. "I would like to stay for a while."

He squeezed her hand. "Good."

For the first time in days, Rachel didn't have the anxious knot in her stomach.

His gaze dropped to her lips. For a moment neither moved. Then, very slowly, he leaned toward her. She didn't retreat.

The kiss was gentle, tentative almost. His lips were soft. They tasted of salt.

She sensed pent-up energy in Ben but he didn't

demand any more of her. It was Rachel who relaxed into the kiss. The black dress slipped from her grasp and fell to the beach.

Footsteps sounded on the narrow beach.

"Ben!"

Ben pulled back seconds before Timothy hurried up to them. The young man's face was flushed, his shirttail out, as if he'd run all the way from the lighthouse.

Embarrassment burned Rachel's cheeks. She felt wanton. She scooped up her dress and stood. She fussed with the buttons on her borrowed jacket as if they'd suddenly become important.

Ben rose slowly. There was no hint of apology in his dark eyes.

Timothy stopped. His gaze darted briefly between the two. "Ben," the young keeper said. He was out of breath, his face flushed. "Bodies from the *Anna St. Claire* have washed up on shore."

Chapter Eight

Ben saw the panic that registered on Rachel's face.

The idea of seeing bodies from any wreck always set his teeth on edge. He'd been a sailor for many years and had served with many good ones. None deserved to end this way—bloated and deformed from their time in the water.

However, finding the bodies from the *Anna St. Claire* meant more to Rachel. They represented a link to a past she desperately wanted to escape.

"Where are they?" Ben said.

The young man's face paled. He'd not seen many dead bodies and the grim task unsettled him. "They washed up about a half mile down the beach."

Ben didn't relish the identification process. He'd seen too many dead seamen this past winter. "How many?"

Timothy swallowed. "Seven."

Rachel smoothed her hands over her hips, clearly nervous. "There were eight men aboard the ship."

"Are you sure?" Ben said.

"Yes, I remember the captain referring to his 'eight-man crew.'"

Ben placed his hand in the small of her back. "That's helpful. Now we know there's only one man missing."

"Will we find the other one?" Timothy asked.

"Hard to say. Often we don't find all the bodies. It's a miracle so many washed up so close to one another."

"The first mate talked about the men lowering the lifeboats," Rachel said.

Ben nodded. "They were likely in the lifeboat together when it capsized."

"By the looks of them, they've been on the beach since last night."

"I'll take Rachel back to the cottage," Ben said. "And then I'll meet you on the beach."

Rachel hesitated. "I'd like to go with you."

Ben squinted into the noonday sun. "It's not a pretty sight."

She lifted her chin. "One of the men has something that belongs to me. It's quite valuable. I'd like it back if it's possible."

He remembered the indention on her ring finger the first night he'd found her. "If there is anything of value on those men, it's long been stripped off by one of the scavengers. But we can check the bodies for it."

She shook her head. "I promise to stay out of your way, but I want to go."

"Suit yourself."

They arrived at the northern section of the beach an hour later. Timothy had recruited two men from town and together they'd led a cart pulled by donkeys up the beach. Rachel walked behind the cart, Ben several paces ahead of everyone.

"I claim the best pair of boots," said a man she'd come to know as Oscar Derbyshire. A grizzled fisherman with stoop shoulders and a deeply wrinkled face, he looked to be past sixty.

"You got the best boots last time," said the younger man next to him. A fisherman, also, Clayton Stump wasn't more than thirty yet his lined face, roughened hands and bent shoulders testified to the countless hours spent handling nets and lures in the hot sun.

The men's attitudes toward the dead was mercenary, yet Rachel couldn't fault them. She'd come for her own selfish reasons. She wanted to know which of the sailors had survived. Captain LaFortune had her ring, the one true link to her past. He and the sailor Rubin had also seen her face.

Ben stopped and held up his hand. Rachel looked up and one hundred feet ahead saw the bodies. Whatever thoughts she'd had of searching for her ring faded. The lifeless forms lying in the sand tore at her. The men had not been reputable, but they had been living, breathing men just days ago and now they were dead.

Grim faced, Ben walked ahead while Rachel and the others waited behind. Timothy looked green, but he started to follow Ben.

Ben turned. "Stay."

"I want to help," Timothy said.

"You will soon enough. Get your bearings first."

The young man nodded, clearly grateful for the reprieve.

Oscar shook his head. "I've collected dozens of bodies in my time and it never gets easy. The sea can do nasty things to a man."

Timothy swallowed.

Ben moved ahead alone. He knelt in front of one body. Using a piece of driftwood, he lifted the man's coat.

"What's he doing?" Rachel said.

Oscar pulled chewing tobacco from his pocket and bit off a piece. "Looking for anything that'll identify the man. Ben likes to notify next of kin if he can."

Though the bodies rested over a hundred feet away, the wind carried the smell of the dead. Rachel's stomach roiled. Clayton leaned against the wagon and shoved his hands into his pockets. "It's a waste of time if you ask me. No one cares about a bunch of sailors."

Oscar spit. "Ben does."

Rachel folded her hands over her chest and watched as Ben moved from man to man, checking pockets. He didn't rush the grim task. Thirty minutes passed before he returned.

Ben nodded to Oscar and Clayton. His face had paled and his expression had tightened. "You can pick them up."

The fisherman nodded and started forward with their cart.

Timothy glanced over at the dead sailors. "You find anything?"

"The redheaded one is named Sebastian. There is another named Michaels and one named Rubin. The rest have nothing on them."

Rubin—the big sailor that had sailed the seas for forty years—was dead. The one that had called her cursed. An unexpected wave of sadness washed over her.

"I don't think the captain is among the dead," Ben said.

"He is a big man with a black beard and a blue vest. His name is Antoine LaFortune," she said.

Ben stared down at her, his expression unreadable. "He wasn't there."

"Do you think that he's alive?" she said.

Ben shrugged but he studied her face closely. "My guess is that he's dead. And that his body will wash up somewhere else on the beach."

Rachel hated the wave of relief that slid through her body.

"He has what you were looking for?"

"Yes."

"Likely then it's lost for good with him."

Rachel stared out at the calm sea. She didn't wish harm to LaFortune, but she prayed her ring rested at the bottom of the ocean.

Ben took her arm. "Let's get back to the cottage."

She offered no argument. "Thank you."

Ben gave the sailors's belongings to Timothy and ordered him to make a note in the keeper's log, while Oscar and Clayton set about the grim task of collecting and burying the bodies.

Taking Rachel's arm, Ben started back toward

the cottage with her. They walked in silence most of the way.

"Have you dealt with many bodies before?" Rachel asked Ben as they approached the cottage.

"Twenty-nine this winter alone." His hands were shoved into his pockets. The wind blew his hair.

"I don't think I'll ever be able to get that sight out of my mind."

"It's a sad part of life here, Rachel."

"When I look at the lighthouse this morning, I thought about rescues, not death."

"There'd be a lot more deaths without the light."

"You make a difference here," she said. "That must feel good."

"On the good days when I can save someone it does. Days like today, I wonder if I'm not fighting an uphill battle."

She laid her hand on his arm. "You're not."

He stopped and stared at her a long moment. Only inches from her, the energy from him felt like a touch.

"My shift doesn't start until sunset," Ben said as they approached the cottage. "There's a tub there if you'd liked to take a bath. I can set it up for you."

Ben could not have given her a greater gift. She wanted nothing more than to wash away the memories of the sailors. "Truly? My skin is coated with salt and sand."

"A good scrubbing will take care of that."

As they walked up the steps, Rachel's spirits buoyed. She breathed deeply, grateful to be alive and, for now, safe.

"I'll fill the tub for you," Ben said.

Rachel followed him up the back steps to the porch and into the kitchen. On the table sat her black dress that she'd dropped off at the cottage before they'd gone to see the bodies. Next to it sat a package wrapped in brown paper.

Attached was a card. Rachel picked up the card and read, "From Ida."

She shrugged off her coat and hung into on a peg next to his. "Ida has sent me a package."

Ben raised an eyebrow. "What is it?"

She undid the twine and unwrapped the brown paper. Inside was the blue ready-made dress. She touched the soft package. "Did you have anything to do with this?"

Ben peered over her shoulder. "No."

"Why would Ida give this to me?"

"I've never known her to give a dress away. I think she has a soft spot for you." Then, as if reading her thoughts, "If you accept the dress, it will mean more to her than you."

Tears choked her throat. Ida understood Rachel as if she'd once been in the same position herself.

"Let's get that bath of yours ready," Ben said.

She wiped a tear from her face. "You don't have to do that for me."

"It's no trouble."

"Just show me where everything is. I'll take care of it." She had a chance to start over and she needed to learn how to live outside her gilded cage. In truth, she didn't know the first thing about caring for herself.

He shoved his fingers through his windswept hair. "You ever filled a bath before?"

Rachel shrugged. "No, but I imagine its not complicated."

He smiled indulgently. "The simplest chores can take hours if you don't know how to do it."

"Good heavens, I'm not helpless." She'd be grateful for a task now. "I can turn the knobs and fill my own tub."

"Trust me," Ben said. "You want me to do this job."

"If you show me to the bathing room, I can take it from there."

"No bathing room here, princess."

"Then where on earth do you keep your tub?"

He went to a small door off the kitchen and

opened it. From a peg on the wall, he pulled down a tin tub and set in the middle of the kitchen. The tub looked more like an oversize bucket.

Amused, Ben raised an eyebrow. "Expecting something a little different?"

She could sit in the tub but she wouldn't be able to stretch out her legs. "It's so small."

He stared at her, amused.

"I'm sorry. I didn't mean to offend."

He grinned. "As long as we're just talking about the tub, none was taken."

The innuendo wasn't lost on her. She'd heard the servants in her father's house often enough. She blushed. "Of course, I referred to the tub."

He laughed. "Don't look so scandalized, princess. I was joking."

Her face grew redder by the minute. She'd never joked with a man before and didn't know what to say. "It won't take long to fill at least."

"Its more work than you're used to, I'll wager."

"I can do it." She glanced around the room and spotted the pots on the stove. "Where's the water?"

"There's a cistern outside," he said patiently.

"Outside."

"Gets better and better, doesn't it?"

He'd read her mind. "No, no, its fine. I should have no problem."

Ben snatched up a pot from the stove. "Come with me."

She followed him outside to a large drum next to the house. "It looks a hundred years old."

"Mental rusts here in a matter of months. It's the salt air. The only fresh water here is rainwater. The cistern catches it."

She watched as he dipped the pot in the water. She looked in the pot. "The water is a little yellow."

"The rust. But its safe."

He carried the bucket inside and placed it on the stove. "Let me fill the others."

"I can do it."

"It's hard work, princess."

"I'm not afraid of work."

He took her hand in his and turned it over. "Not one callus. Lily-white."

Shivers danced down her spine. "Its time they had a few calluses."

He traced his finger over a small scar that hooked around her thumb. "How'd you get this?"

She'd cut it when Peter had forced her to pick up a broken tumbler he'd smashed against the wall.

Rachel pulled her hand away, curling her fingers over the scar. "I was careless."

He held her fist in his hand. "I doubt you had a careless day in your life."

She saw the questions in his eyes. "I need to get ready for my bath."

He shrugged. "How about I hang around while you fill the tub, just in case it's more work than you realized."

"That's not necessary."

"It is to me."

The quiet determination in his words touched her. She tore her gaze from his. "It's no great mystery. Fill the pot with water and heat it." She went to the stove and picked up an empty pot. The pot weighed more than she'd imagined. Ben had made it look so effortless.

The bucket thumped against the side of the stove and then her legs as she pulled it off the stove. Her life had changed forever and the time had arrived for her to learn independence. However, it would have been nicer to tackle this little task without an audience.

Pot in hand, she headed out the back door to the cistern. She dunked the bucket in the water but discovered that with it full, it was too heavy to lift.

"Good Lord, it weighs a ton."

"Had enough?" Ben said.

The wind had swept his black hair over his eyes. He looked quite handsome.

She blew a strand of hair out of her eyes. "No.

One way or another I'll get the pot inside." The pot handle bit into her fingers as she tried to lift it.

"Maybe, but I'll be damned if I'll stand here on my afternoon off and watch you break your back." He took the pot from her and carried it inside.

She followed behind him. "I need to learn these things, if I am to be a strong, independent woman."

"A bucket of water and a wrenched back won't prove anything." He set the pot on the stove. "It'll be an hour before the water's warm enough."

"An hour?" For years she'd ordered baths without a second thought.

"I'll get you soap and towels from my room." He strode out before she commented.

"I can at least do that."

"Please sit. Next time," he said.

Rachel sat at the kitchen table and began to unwind the long braid that hung down her back. She combed her fingers through her thick mane of hair. It would take at least an hour to work the knots from it.

"I brought a comb," he said, returning. He set the towels and soap on the table. "Figured you could use it."

"Thank you. You must be a mind reader."

Rachel ran her hand through her hair. It felt greasy and smelled of seaweed. The long tresses were a thick mass. It needed washing but she dreaded the task. It would take hours for her hair to fully dry. Untangling the knots would take time.

"Can't say when I've ever seen so much hair on a woman's head." He went to the stove and poured himself a mug of coffee.

Rachel started to work the comb through her hair. The comb snagged in her tangles, painfully tugging her scalp. "I've never cut it."

He stared at her over the rim of his cup. "Never?"

Rachel cursed the tangles. "I've wanted to a hundred times, believe me." Until now she didn't mind that her hair was long. "There's always been a maid to brush and braid it."

"I've scissors if you want to shear some of that off."

The comb caught in another knot. "I couldn't cut it."

"Why not?"

"There are a thousand reasons."

"Name one."

Peter wouldn't like it. She stopped, furious with herself. Peter didn't matter anymore. He was the past.

So why couldn't she cut it? "I suppose there's no reason not to take a little off." Still, the idea of cutting her hair had her heart pounding.

"I'll get the scissors." He took a sip of coffee, set the mug down and ambled into the other room. Less than a minute later he returned with the scissors. He handed them to her. "Cut away."

He looked so casual, as if this weren't a big deal.

She stared down at the blades. They felt heavy in her hands. Of course, this wasn't a big deal, especially after what they'd witnessed on the beach today. Hair, after all, would grow back.

Grabbing a clump of hair just below her shoulder, she raised the scissors to the tangles.

She hesitated. Suddenly she was afraid. There were so many changes in her life. She was literally cutting away the person she'd been. She lowered the scissors from her hair.

"What's keeping you?" Ben said.

Tears sprang to her eyes. "I don't know. I'm being silly. In truth I've wanted to cut my hair for years."

"You want me to do it?"

"You cut a woman's hair?"

"We're only talking about cutting a straight line, right?"

"Yes."

"It shouldn't be that difficult."

"I don't know." Good Lord, what would she look like after Ben finished with her?

He held out his hand. "You want it done or not?"

"Yes. Yes, I want my hair cut." She laid the scissors in his hand.

When he took them, his fingers brushed hers and fire shot through her limbs.

He moved behind her chair. She could feel the heat of his body. Nervous energy shot through her body. "Now, don't take too much off."

"You've got enough here to make a rug. You could stand to lose a foot or two," he teased.

Suddenly she had a vision of him cutting it at her ears. "Maybe this isn't such a good idea."

"Afraid, Rachel?"

She hesitated. "No." She squeezed her eyes closed. "Go ahead."

He grabbed a handful of hair and in one swift move, cut the golden strands. He handed her the hair. "No so bad was it?"

For a moment she sat in shocked horror staring at the large clump of hair in her hand. "You cut it!"

"That's what you wanted."

She took the hair and looked at it. It had been with her for so long. "Yes, but I didn't think you'd do it so *fast*. I thought you'd give me a little more time to think about it."

He lifted a brow. "It's best to get the harder things over and done with quickly."

Her hair now dangled just below her shoulders. Her head felt light. "How does it look?"

"Crooked."

"How crooked?"

"Nothing I can't trim up." He spread a towel over her shoulders and spent the next fifteen minutes snipping away at the ends of her hair. The extra time gave her the chance to calm her nerves and get accustomed to her shorter hairstyle.

As Ben trimmed, he cupped her chin and turned her head to inspect a cut. His touch wasn't gentle, but rough and slightly awkward. Yet each time his fingers brushed her skin, her nerves sizzled. The heat of his body burned into her skin. She was aware of his breath; the frown that creased his brown when he inspected his work. Soon she forgot the hair and became aware only of him.

"Done," he said.

He had a satisfied smile on his face.

"Looks good," he said

She ran her hand through her hair, amazed how light it felt. "It feels short."

"Too damn much hair, if you ask me. Must have felt like you had a sheep dog on your head at times."

She laughed. In truth the weight sometimes gave her headaches. "Yes."

With her hair gone, she felt like a different woman. Freer.

"The water should be hot," he said. "I'll pour it in the tub for you." He started to fill the tub. "It's amazing to me you could wash your hair."

"There was always a maid to help me."

"Come over here and kneel by the tub and I'll pour water over your head. It'll be easier to clean it that way."

"I'm sure I can manage now that it's shorter."

"It'll be easier, if I help."

He looked so masculine standing there with his sleeves rolled up over this elbows. The thought of him touching her again was exciting. Dangerous.

Still, she knelt over the tub. She flipped her hair over as he came to stand beside her. In her peripheral vision she saw his powerful legs braced beside her.

He brushed his hands through her hair, away from her collar. Slowly he poured the water over her head, working the water through the thick tresses with his hand. "Hold still while I get the soap."

He rubbed the soap between his hands and began to work it into her scalp. His hands possessed such strength, yet they were gentle.

The sensation was so pleasurable. He poured a fresh pitcher of water over her head, working all the soap out of her hair. He wrapped a towel over her head. "All set."

Boneless, she rose. Water dripped down the sides of her face. "Wonderful."

He backed away as if he needed distance. He filled the tub with the remaining hot water. "I'll leave you to your bath."

After Ben left, Rachel stripped off her clothes and eased into the hot water. She couldn't stretch out in the tub, but the hot water soothed her aching muscles.

She stayed in the tub until the water had nearly cooled. When she got out, she felt refreshed—a new woman.

She looked at her black dress. It conjured memories of Peter and the fear she'd felt when she'd run away. Her gaze shifted to the parcel. Accepting a parcel from a near stranger wasn't proper.

"Proper," she muttered. "What have you done these last three days that is proper?"

Rachel pulled out the blue dress. It felt soft against her skin. The color caught the light.

She put on the chemise, stockings, new dress and shoes. To her delight, it all fit perfectly. The clothes were plain but comfortable. They felt good against her skin. She felt like a different person.

She moved into the parlor. The room was filled

with a half dozen unpacked crates. Not one picture hung on the wall. But Ben had laid a fire in the hearth and pulled the one settee close to it.

Touched by his kindness, she sat and started to comb her wet hair. The comb slid easily through her mane, which had already started to dry and curl at the ends. This place was magical.

A place to start over.

Peter slammed his hand on the mahogany table. "What do you mean, she's disappeared? She's a well-known woman for God's sake. Someone must have seen her."

The three detectives stood stone-faced. "We've checked all the passenger boats and the coaches. No one has seen her."

White-hot rage thrummed through Peter's veins.

Damn her! If it took him the rest of his life, he'd find Rachel and teach her a lesson.

"Well, check them again," Peter shouted. "If you hope to work in this town ever again, you will find my wife!"

The tallest of the detectives stepped forward. "We've not checked the freighters, but it's unlikely a lady alone would dare a crossing with rough sailors."

Peter's eyes narrowed. Rachel wouldn't be so

foolish. Would she? But then until now he'd assumed she'd acted alone. What if she had run with someone? A lover perhaps? "Check them."

The detective shrugged. "That will be easy enough. A woman on a freighter will be remembered."

"Good do it!"

The men left him alone in his office. He started to pace. But the anger and restlessness inside him boiled in his veins. He'd given Rachel everything. He'd cared for her and loved her when she had no one. And this was how she repaid her.

In his heart he knew she'd taken a lover. She'd never have had the courage to run on her own. She was too weak. Chances were they were in bed together now laughing at him.

Peter picked up a crystal paperweight and hurled it across the room. It smashed against the hearth.

"Damn you, Rachel!"

If it took him the rest of his life, he'd find Rachel and teach her a lesson.

Chapter Nine

Ben wasn't prepared for the kick in his gut when he saw Rachel as she stepped outside onto the dunes.

She wore the blue wool dress and white shawl that Ida had given her. The garment hugged her narrow waist and full breasts. Her hair hung loosely at her shoulders, curling up at the edges and catching the sunshine like wheat on a winter day. The wind brushed the hem of her skirt, revealing slim ankles. Simple but stunning.

Rachel saw him, waved and smiled. The lifeless woman he'd pulled from the *Anna St. Claire* had vanished.

Ben waved back. The gesture was casual; he felt anything but. If he had his way, he'd take Rachel back to the cottage, lock out the world and spend the next five days making love to her.

Frustrated, he turned away from her. "Timothy, let's get the boat to the surf," he said, his voice gruff.

They were hauling the dory to the beach. The *Anna St. Claire* remained half submerged in the water just beyond the surf.

Timothy gripped the edge of the boat. "What's wrong with you?"

"Nothing."

"You look angry."

Ben's muscles bunched as he started to drag the boat. "I'm fine."

"So, why are we going to the wreck again?"

"To inspect the salvage operation."

"Do you do that a lot?"

"No."

"Then why now?"

"Damn boy, you could talk the balls off a brass monkey."

Timothy laughed. "She looks good cleaned up, if you ask me," he said as he helped drag the boat.

Ben glared at the younger man. He didn't question the possessiveness thrumming in his veins. He wanted Rachel for himself. "Keep those thoughts to yourself."

"What thoughts?" he said, grinning. "Hey, I'll be a married man in just a few days. It's the rest of the men in the village you should be worrying about."

"She's off-limits to everyone."

Timothy's eyes gleamed. "Why do you care?"

"Because I do."

Timothy lifted an eyebrow. "Since when?"

"Since now."

They reached the surf and Timothy wound the rope into a neat circle. "I saw Callie a few minutes ago. She had more details about the wedding." The boy rolled his eyes, as if exasperated by all the details a woman could attach to a simple ceremony. "Anyway, she's invited Rachel."

"She might not be here tomorrow."

Timothy shook his head. "We're going out to the wreck because of Rachel."

There were better reasons to go to the wreck. Too many villagers, eager for the bounty, drowned on unstable wrecks. But the truth was he was going today for Rachel. He didn't expect to find luggage—likely Rachel didn't have any. Runaways usually didn't. "That's right."

"Why?"

Ben shoved out a sigh. "She left her purse behind. It has all her money in it. I thought I'd check to see if I could find it." He didn't want anyone else finding this last link to her past. Once he'd returned the purse, he told himself he would let go of her past if she stayed.

"You're bitten."

They pushed the boat into the surf and jumped in. Ben dug the oars into the water. "What the devil are you talking about?"

"You got it bad for Rachel. Just like I do for Callie."

"I don't know what I have," he said. And maybe that was what was eating at him so much.

"The ladies in the village won't like this. They've got their minds set that you'll marry one of their daughters. You've been linked to Molly enough."

He hadn't missed the not-so-subtle attempts of the women, the parade of cakes and the endless questions when he walked into the village last fall. Molly had always offered a good laugh, but he'd never pictured her rocking his babies to sleep. But he could see Rachel with his children. "She's still set on leaving."

Timothy shook his head. "Maybe that's for the best. She's a looker but a bit cold for my tastes."

Ben had felt her heat and energy when he'd washed her hair. She'd moaned with pleasure as he'd worked the soap into her scalp. The sound had made him grow hard.

"She isn't cold. It's fear that has kept her reserved."

"Fear of what?"

"I don't know." He glanced over his shoulder at the wreck. "Do me a favor?"

"Anything."

"When you go to the mainland and send that telegram about the *Anna St. Claire,* don't mention Rachel."

"There could be people looking for her."

"I know there are people looking for her. That's what's scaring her."

Timothy squinted against the sun. "You sure you want to get involved in whatever trouble she's running from?"

That very question had kept him up last night. "If she's willing to stay, I'm willing."

Timothy chuckled.

"What's so funny?" Irritation snapped in his voice.

"It's what Ida told me when I proposed to my Callie after only three days of courting."

"What's that?"

"You're thinking with the wrong head."

Ben smiled. "I'm a bit older than you, lad. I'm thinking with my big head." Though the smaller one was doing its fair share of driving.

Angry voices of the scavengers carried over the water. "We better get out there," Ben said. "Sounds like we've got a fight brewing."

"The rumors about the *Anna St. Claire* are flying. It's said that Captain LaFortune was carrying gold."

Ben muttered an oath. "That rumor flies every time we have a wreck. But speaking of Captain La-Fortune, has there been any sign of him?"

"Not a one," Timothy said. "Do you think he survived?"

"Who's to say? Stranger things have happened. If he didn't, we might not ever know."

Together they started to drag the boat across the sand. The wind from the ocean whipped around them.

Ben glanced toward the wreck. The boat listed badly to the right but the hull still held. A wrecked ship could vanish from sight in a matter of hours whereas some lingered for weeks.

A collection of small boats circled. The boats were loaded and headed to shore. A few men still remained on deck. They'd set about stripping everything that wasn't nailed down. He recognized Clayton and Oscar. They had gotten to work on a small cannon fastened to the deck.

Wrecked ships served as an industry of sorts in this area. Many families made their living harvesting and then selling what they found.

Timothy helped Ben drag the dory to the edge

of the water. He hopped in. "She'll be lost to the sea in a day or two."

"Aye." Ben pushed the boat onto the surface. The waves splashed against his worn boots.

Time was running out. If Rachel left any clues to her past, now was the time find them.

With clear skies and calm weather, he and Timothy glided across the waters toward the *Anna St. Claire*. They reached the ship five minutes later.

"Hard to believe we rowed out to the same boat just three nights ago," Timothy said. "I don't mind telling you I was scared out of my wits."

Ben nodded to a fisherman lowering one of the *Anna St. Claire*'s canvas sails into his boat. "A bit of fear is good. It keeps you on your toes."

They moored alongside the wreck just as they had done days ago. Ben grabbed onto a stretch of rope one of the scavengers was using. He tugged on it to make sure it held secure.

"Want to come up?"

Timothy glanced up at the ship. "Doesn't look so frightening as she did before."

Ben grinned. "No ghosts, I'll wager."

Timothy's cheeks colored with embarrassment. "What are the chances of you finding anything?"

"Poor." But he needed to look.

He hoisted himself on board. Horace Freely, a fisherman, stood on the deck. A big man, with a round belly, he sported a full red beard. He wore a stocking cap and a pea jacket over his dark pants. His boots were scuffed.

Next to him stood Steve Jenkins. Tall and thin, he was young, not more than thirty, but his shoulders slumped—evidence of his twenty years hauling nets full of fish.

Both men look angry. Each held opposite ends of the boat's wheel.

"You said I could have it," Horace said.

Steve tightened his grip. "You got the wheel on the last ship."

"What's going on, men?" Ben asked.

Both looked up at him, surprised to see him.

"Ain't never seen you two on a wreck before," Horace said. "What brings you out here?"

Ben stood with his feet braced apart on the sloping ship. To his surprise, she'd not shifted much in the past couple of days. "Hoping to retrieve a few of Rachel's belongings."

Horace yanked the wheel out of Steve's hands. "If she left it belowdecks, you'll never find it."

Steve glared at Horace. Their argument for the wheel hadn't ended. "It's completely flooded. I tried to swim down there myself but it's pitch black."

Horace and Steve couldn't swim like many of the other fishermen. However, Ben was a powerful swimmer. After his parents had died, he had pestered Ida until she'd found someone to teach him how to swim. He'd sensed then that the ocean would always be a part of his life and he'd wanted every advantage he could muster when he dealt with her. Timothy's ability to swim had been one of the reasons he'd okayed his hire.

Ben glanced toward the small door that led to the hold belowdecks. "I may have a look anyway."

Horace scratched his chin. "We'll help if you give us half of what you find."

"Thanks, but no. Timothy and I will see to it."

The two men nodded but neither looked happy. They wanted the bounty belowdecks and were frustrated that they couldn't get to it.

Ben and Timothy walked to the door. Water slashed over the steps. Rays of sunshine from the cracked deck above seeped through the hallway ceiling.

Timothy squatted and looked below. He shook his head. "Where did you find Rachel?"

Ben shrugged off his jacket. "The cabin on the right."

Timothy squinted. "A miracle you found her."

"Aye." Finding her had been a hurdle but he suspected keeping her would be an even greater one.

"You know if you find her money, there won't be anything to keep her from leaving," Timothy said.

"I want her to stay because she wants to, not because she has to."

"And how are you ever gonna find it?"

"I'll have a look and see if I get lucky."

Ben took the rope from Timothy and tied one end around his waist. "If I tug on it, I've got a problem."

"I'll come after you if I feel the tug."

Ben clamped his hand on Timothy's shoulder. He'd not started shaving, yet in this moment he spoke like a man of great confidence. "Just pull me out."

Rechecking the line, Ben took in a deep breath and then slipped below the water's surface. Salt water stung his eyes and blurred his vision, but he cut through the water, knowing he'd have about a minute before he had to resurface for air. He reached the cabin easily. The door he'd chopped through nights ago still hung on the hinges.

He swam into the small cabin. Because of the angle of the ship, this side faced up. Though flooded, bits of light filtered in through the portal.

A chair floated in the corner above three wine crates. Next to the bunk, he saw the purse. It floated in the water, its mother-of-pearl beading flickering in the light.

He grabbed the purse and shoved it in his belt. He untied the rope from his waist and fastened it to each of the crates. The wine would be a welcome edition at Callie and Timothy's wedding.

When he reached the surface, his lungs ached for air. Timothy waited for him. He'd taken off his coat as if he were ready to dive into the water.

"I thought I'd have to come in after you."

Ben gasped in another lungful of air. "I found you a wedding gift. Tug on the line."

Timothy pulled the rope and the three crates of wine appeared. He dragged the crates up to the top deck and pulled out a bottle. "This has the look of expensive wine."

Ben shook off the damp water. "I think that it is."

"Did you find the purse?"

Ben tugged the delicate bag from his belt. In the sunlight he could see that it was finely made, very expensive. "Aye."

In the handle were carved the initials R.E. Who the devil was R.E.?

"You going to open it?"

He touched the clasp with his thumb, rubbed his

finger over the engraved lettering. "I'm tempted, but no, I won't open it."

"Yeah, but how are you going to find out anything more about Rachel if you don't open it?"

"I'll wait until she tells me."

Rachel stood on the beach as Ben and Timothy rowed the last wave in. The waves crashed around them as they hopped out of the boat in the knee-deep water and pulled the dory to shore. Boxes filled the boat.

She hugged her shawl around her shoulders. Ben's hair was wet as were his pants and the shirt under his jacket. A jolt of worry snapped through her body.

Rachel met them at the water's edge. She was careful to stay out of the surf and to keep her boots dry. "What happened?"

Ben's gaze caught hers. Dark and hot, it sent rivulets of desire through her. "No, trouble," he said. "Just doing a bit of scavenging."

Timothy grinned. "He found three cases of wine on the *Anna St. Claire.* Said me and Callie could use them for our wedding."

She glanced at Ben, wondering why he'd venture to the ship. "What a wonderful gift for you."

Timothy picked up a crate. "Is it any good?

Rachel lifted a bottle. "Ah, yes, this is very fine indeed. It's a French red. The year is excellent and you'll find the taste not too sweet or bitter."

The boy shrugged. "I'm an ale man myself."

Rachel knew fine wines, Ben mused. Another detail to add to his meager collection of information he knew about her. "Why don't you get those boxes up to the boathouse?"

"Oh, yeah, sure. Be back in a minute for the others." He hurried away.

Ben pulled the boat away from the surf.

"You found the wine in the captain's cabin," Rachel said.

"Sitting right there by the bunk without a one broken."

"When you spoke of the scavengers before, there was an edge of distaste in your voice. You're not the kind of man that goes back for a case of wine."

He unloaded the two remaining cases and set them on the beach. "I didn't go back for the wine."

"Then what?"

He reached under his coat and pulled out her purse. He laid the purse in her hand. "This."

"Why would you take such a risk?"

"I'm assuming there were no trunks to be found in the hold of the ship."

She fingered the mother-of-pearl design. "No, there weren't."

"Then you hold all the connections to your past."

"Why?"

"You've a chance for a fresh start now, Rachel." His expression was unreadable. "Didn't you say it had all your money?"

"Yes, it does."

He moved closer to her. "Open it."

Tearing her gaze from his, she snapped open the purse. Tucked inside were the wet bills and the volume of poems her mother had given her.

He glanced at the purse. "It should all dry in the sun."

Tears sprang in her eyes. "This is the kindest thing anyone has ever done for me."

He lifted his gaze to hers. They'd darkened with an unreadable emotion. Slowly he leaned forward until his lips almost touched hers. "I want you to stay," he said, his voice hoarse. "But I want you to have a choice."

He brushed a curl from her face. Her smooth skin felt so good against his skin. For a moment they stood on the shore, her skirts moving in the breeze, flapping around his legs. He cupped her face in his hand.

Ben leaned his head forward. He was going to kiss her.

She didn't pull away. The kiss was gentle and undemanding yet it rattled his senses. His body craved more.

She pulled back. "What do you want from me?"

"Stay for a while. Let's see what there is between us."

She twisted one of the shawl tassels around her finger. "I can't make promises to you and I don't want you to make any to me in return."

A smile tipped the edge of his lips. "My promises come with no strings and I give them as I see fit."

As the sun dipped into the horizon twenty miles north on the tiny Virginia costal town, orange-red light splashed over the piers jutting out from the mainland into the ocean. The fishermen, returning from their twelve-hour day at sea, were in good spirits. The catch had been unusually high.

All the boats had returned to port except one—Marcus Smith's. He'd gone out farther today than the other fisherman because he'd wanted to double his catch.

A few fishermen had started to whisper that Marcus might have run into trouble. Boats capsized and fisherman died on clear days.

However, Marcus's older brother didn't listen to the whispers. He had already unloaded their catch for the day. His stomach grumbled and he wanted to get home to his wife. But the brothers had made a pact years ago—they went home together each night.

When Sam spotted Marcus's boat sails, it was past five o'clock. His brother waited until the fishing boat scraped alongside the dock and he could see with his own eyes that his brother faired well until he released a sigh.

"Ahoy, there," Marcus called. "I've found a man!"

The fisherman didn't hurry. Sailors had been found before floating in the ocean. The Atlantic's graveyard claimed many a tall sailing ship.

Sam strode to the end of the dock. Hands on hips, he looked down and studied the man lying in the bottom of the boat on a pile of fish. "Is he dead?"

Tying his boat to the pier, Marcus shook his head. "Wasn't the last time I looked." He nudged the large man with the tip of his boat. "Takes up too much space, if you ask me. I could've caught more fish if I hadn't found him."

Seaweed coated the unconscious man's black beard and his blue jacket now torn at the shoulder. He coughed and sat up with a jerk.

The stranger swung at Marcus's booted foot. "*Merde.* God's curse on you all!"

The brothers nodded. "Alive."

Marcus poked the man again. "Fine talk. I just hauled your worthless ass out of the water."

The man spit. "I might as well be at the bottom. My ship's gone."

Marcus's back ached and he had little patience. "Ships are lost in these waters all the time. You should have been more careful."

Sam offered a hand to the stranger. He wanted to be done with him. "What's your name?"

The man accepted it and climbed up onto the pier. "LaFortune. Captain LaFortune."

Chapter Ten

An hour later Rachel stood on the back porch, watching Ben stride toward the boathouse. Cold sea spray misted her face. The wind flapped her skirts.

His sleeves were rolled up, revealing strong forearms. Muscles bunched and strained as he shoved the boat into the boathouse. The boat looked heavy, yet he moved it with ease.

He'd sent her back to the cottage promising to meet her inside soon. She'd wanted to stay on the beach but understood he had work to do…and she needed to keep her distance.

She glanced down at the soaked purse. Deep conflicting emotions ran through her body.

Ben had given her a gift more valuable than diamonds.

Her father would never have considered him as a suitor. In fact she wouldn't have, either, two years ago. In those days money and social position had seemed so important. She'd learned since then that money and smooth manners could hide a lot of sins.

However her sentiments for Ben went beyond gratitude. He evoked emotions she could not quite define. Seductive and dangerous, warm and tender, her newfound feelings left her afraid and excited.

Like it or not, she cared for him.

Ben tied the boat down and closed up the shed door, taking care to secure the lock. Before Rachel, he'd have spent the several hours before his shift working. Now, he wanted to spend the time with her.

He saw her standing at the kitchen window. Walking faster, he moved across the yard and into the house. Anticipation warmed his blood. The aroma of coffee greeted him.

"You must be frozen to the bone," she said. She stood by the stove peering into the large coffeepot.

The wind had blown her hair free of the ribbon at the nape of her neck, leaving wisps framing her face. The shorter style suited her. She looked much younger. Carefree almost.

For the first time, the cottage felt like home. "I'm used to the cold. Is that coffee?"

"It's the same from this morning but I've managed to warm it. Though it's so strong you might need a take a fork and knife to it."

"That kind of coffee builds character." He saw the purse lying on the table. His gaze scanned the initials on the handle. R.E. "You should open the bag. Let the bills dry."

She nodded. "You're right. I'd meant to open it, but it took me longer than I thought to stoke the fire to heat the coffee."

He accepted the cup she offered. His fingers brushed hers. "Have you ever laid a fire in a stove before?"

"No," she said, laughing. "Luck led me to the kindling trap and glowing embers."

He watched her move to the table. He waited, expecting something. What that something was, he couldn't say.

She pulled out the roll of bills and a small leather-bound volume. She reached not for the bills, but for the book. Salt water stained the leather-bound cover and the pages had all but dissolved into each other. Gently she opened the book. It was ruined.

Rachel tipped back her head. To his surprise he saw tears pool.

"What is it?" he said.

"A book of poems." She wiped away a tear.

He stared at her, baffled by her sadness. "Your money seems to be all here."

"Yes."

Any practical-minded woman would see that the money was paramount. "You're crying."

She turned her face from his. "I'm not."

He laid a land on her shoulder. "I don't know much about women and their emotions, but I know crying when I see it. What's wrong?"

"I'm being silly. It's just that I loved this book."

He glanced down at a soggy volume. "You can buy others one day."

She gently turned a soggy page. It tore. "It wouldn't quite be the same."

"A book's a book."

"It was a gift from my mother. She gave it to me on my twelfth birthday. The cancer took her just months later." Rachel reverently closed the book. "I've read a poem in the book every day since. It's a great source of comfort. I can't believe that I hadn't thought about it these last couple of days." She gently laid the book on the table. "This book was my only friend at times."

"Why were you so alone?"

For a moment she stood silent, staring at the book, then she stared up at him, her eyes liquid sapphires. "Kiss me."

"What?"

"Kiss me."

He took a small step toward her, closing the gap between them. He waited, ready to back off if she looked skittish.

But she didn't back away. Her gaze lifted to his lips. She was curious about him. "I want to taste you again."

Ben needed no further encouragement. He tipped her chin up as he lowered his head toward hers. She closed her eyes. He hovered close to her, his lips only inches from her. Lord, but he liked just looking at her. Slowly he closed the inches between them and pressed his lips to hers.

She tasted sweet. Like nectar. And he quickly discovered that one chaste kiss would never be enough. He banded his hand around her waist and gently pulled her close. He deepened the kiss. She melted against him, her arms wrapping around his neck.

He struggled to keep a rein on his desires. He wanted nothing more than to take her to his room and drive into her.

She rose up on tiptoes, sliding her long fingers into his hair.

He hugged her closer to him. He coaxed her lips open with his tongue and explored the soft folds of her mouth.

A soft, mewing sound rumbled in her throat. His body hardened in response. He'd never wanted a woman more than Rachel.

But the mysteries surrounding Rachel hovered in his mind. He wanted to pretend the past didn't exist but the unknown cut through the haze of desire. His body still raged for her, but his mind rebelled.

As much as he wanted her, he sensed if he took her now he'd lose her.

He broke the kiss.

He kept his hands on her narrow waist, but put a few inches between them. He stared at her closed eyes and her lips still moist from the kiss.

Her eyes fluttered open. Embarrassment colored her cheeks when she realized he was staring at her. Slowly, she unwound her hands from around his neck. "Did I do something wrong?"

"No." His voice sounded ragged.

"Then why did you stop? Am I not good at this?"

Dear Lord, didn't she realize she had the power to make his knees weak? "I want you to kiss me because you want to, not because you're trying to shut me up."

She blinked stunned. "I wasn't—"

"You were," he interrupted. "And I happily obliged. But it won't work next time, Rachel. Next

time I ask a question about your past, don't sub-
stitute answers with kisses." Without another word
he left.

The early-morning sun sent light streaming into
the kitchen. Rachel swirled the remains of her tea
in the white porcelain cup. She'd not slept well
last night. She'd dreamed of monsters, Ben and
destruction.

The wind scraped a tree branch against the window in the parlor. She started, then felt a fool for
having the jitters.

She set her cup down on the kitchen counter.
For a few hours yesterday, she'd tried to pretend
that the past didn't exist. Like a fool, she'd heated
the coffee as if she had a right to him. She'd even
been humming.

But when she'd opened the purse, the past had
come crashing back and wedged itself between
Ben and her.

Ben had been right. Initially, desire hadn't
driven her kiss. She kissed him out of fear. She
wanted to keep the fantasy alive and to forget.

But the kiss had quickly changed from a diver-
sion to something much more intense.

She remembered the feel of his lips against
hers. His kiss had been soft, gentle, but she'd
tasted the passion that coursed through his body.

He'd wanted more. And God help her, she'd have gladly given him more. His touch made her body sing. He ignited a heat in her that had grown cold long ago.

And then he'd pulled away.

Rachel closed her eyes. Ridiculous to think she could deceive him and herself. She was shackled to a past that would never leave her in peace.

She had her money now. And it truly wasn't safe to stay. In time someone would get word to Peter that she had survived the wreck. The allure of his wealth seduced everyone eventually. Hadn't that been the reason she'd married him—for security?

She paced. The sooner she left this place, the better. Ben and everyone else here would be better off once she'd gone. Peter would raze the village if he found her here.

Her mind set, she went to her bedroom to retrieve her possessions. She changed out of the blue wool dress and into her black traveling dress. Folding the blue dress neatly, she laid it on his bed. She tucked the volume of poems in her reticule and stashed her money in her corset.

Rachel paused at the threshold and looked back at the simple room. It had been a haven. If not for Ben and the shelter of this room, she would have died.

Ben's promises to keep her safe were true and

honorable. But Peter would punish Ben for harboring her and she couldn't bear that thought.

She swallowed the lump in her throat and closed the bedroom door.

Moving into the kitchen, she pulled on her coat. Once she reached the village, she'd find Ida. Without words, the woman understood her plight. She'd help Rachel.

Rachel glanced up at the lighthouse. Ben had not extinguished the lanterns. The tower light burned bright against the thickening clouds behind it.

She did not like sneaking off like this, but there could be no other way. Ben would try to stop her. And she might very well be tempted to stay.

Turning away, she started down the narrow sandy path that cut through the wind-bent trees. She reached the village in fifteen minutes.

The town was quiet, the streets and the boardwalk empty. Good, Rachel thought. The less attention to her departure, the better.

The weather had shifted since last night. Colder, the wind bit through her coat and chilled her skin. She wasted no time getting to Ida's shop. The bells above the mercantile door jangled as she entered.

Ida stood behind the counter. She glanced up at her over a stack of canned of peaches. "Morning."

Rachel moved down the narrow center row lined with barrels of whiskey and sacks of flour and salt. Above her head hung baskets and dried herbs. "I want to thank you for the dress."

Ida's gaze swept over Rachel, taking in the black dress. "That why you came?"

"I need to see Sloan about a ride to the mainland."

Ida lifted a brow. "I thought you might be staying with us for a while."

Rachel's stomach clenched. "It's best that I leave."

Ida frowned. "All right, I'll walk you over to his dock as soon as I unpack this box. Have a seat."

She clutched her belongings. "If you'll just show me the way. You don't have to come."

Ida continued to stack cans of peaches, but her voice had an edge to it now. "Have you talked to Ben about this change of heart?"

"No. He wouldn't understand."

Ida wiped her hands on her apron and came out from behind the counter. "He wants you to stay."

Tightness banded around Rachel's chest. "I know."

"He can keep you safe," Ida said softly.

Rachel didn't hide her confusion. "You've wanted me to leave from the start. Why the change?"

Ida stacked another can. "I've seen the way Ben looks at you. He's not looked at another woman like that before. For the last few days, he's been happy. That means a lot to me."

"Ida, someone's looking for me. He will destroy this town if he finds out you've been harboring me."

Ida's gaze was as direct as Ben's. "Ben has weathered some terrible storms before. He doesn't scare easily."

"This time he should."

"This person is no match for Ben."

Rachel admired Ida's pride in Ben. "This person is very powerful."

"Don't underestimate my Ben. He has never run from a fight. In fact, there are times when I wished he had." Bitterness coated Ida's words.

Her shoulders sagged. "Ben deserves more than I can give. I can't make him any promises. I wish that I could but I can't."

"Ben doesn't except anything from you."

She remembered the kiss. He'd ended it. He wanted *more.*

Ida lifted another box onto the counter. She started to unpack it. "So where will you go?"

Rachel turned and stared out the store's large, glass front window at the gray sky. At the far end of the town, a group of children walked from the docks. "I don't know."

"Not much of a plan."

Children's laughter rang like church bells. Rachel's heart tightened. There'd been a time when she'd dreamed of children. But that dream, like all the others, would never be. "As long as I keep moving, I will be safe."

"You'll be a moving target."

"I've cut my hair and I've gotten sun on my face. If I head inland away from the ports, no one will recognize me."

"You will stick out wherever you go. Poise and quality are hard to hide."

Ida came around the counter toward Rachel. It struck her then that the older woman was shorter than her. Ida possessed an energy that made her seem so much taller. "Sloan just returned from the mainland with the children. But he'll make a trip back if you wish."

Rachel hesitated. Children and parents emerged from the path that led to the Sound. A mother picked up a redheaded girl and swung her around. Both were laughing.

"Mr. Sloan must have left before dawn."

"Folks were anxious to have their children home."

"Where were they?"

"They board on the mainland during the week so they can go to school. Sloan brings them back. They're getting a good education, but the time from their families is hard on everyone."

"My father sent me away to school after my mother died." Her days away at boarding school had been long and lonely. Because she'd boarded in New York, she'd been unable to come home on the winter and spring holidays, just summers.

"Ah." Silence hung between them.

"Why don't you have a school in the village?"

"There's no one to teach the children. Most of us don't have the education to teach them properly. We've tried to hire teachers but none wish to live in such a bleak place."

"This land is rough, but it's lovely."

"I think so, but few outsiders share that opinion."

A young boy, no more than six, ran up to his father. The father picked up the boy, hugging him close. Tears glistened on the father's face.

"How long have the children been gone?" Rachel said.

"Three weeks."

"Why so long?"

"The weather's been too bad to risk a crossing."

"When will they leave?"

"If the weather holds, Sunday afternoon."

Rachel watched a child cup her mother's face. Memories of her mother were vague now. Perfume, soft skin, lullabies.

"Knowing Ben, he will follow you," Ida said.

Panic flared inside her. "He wouldn't!"

"He would. He has set his mind to protect you."

Pride had her lifting her chin. "I don't want to be taken care of like a child."

"Then show some spine, girl. Don't be a weak-willed ninny."

Anger flared. "I'm not weak-willed."

Ida met her gaze. "Then take a stand and stay. This is your chance to recapture your life and start over."

"I don't know how to live in this world."

"Those details have a way of taking care of themselves. All you have to do now is say yes."

Rachel was touched. "Why are you so kind to me?"

Ida shrugged. "I'm not just doing this for you. I'm thinking of Ben."

Footsteps sounded on the boardwalk. The door to the shop jerked open. It was Ben.

His face was tight with tension, until he saw her standing in the store. He released a breath before he reached for the front door.

The bells jingled over his head. "I saw you leave," he said.

Rachel felt the sweep of emotion as she stared at Ben. His raven hair was wind-blown and his collar upturned.

"Rachel and I were just having a visit, weren't we?"

"Yes," she said. Like it or not, she couldn't leave this place now. She was bound to it and to Ben in ways she couldn't begin to describe.

Chapter Eleven

A heavy silence hung between Rachel and Ben as they walked back to the lighthouse. A scowl darkened Ben's face. Rachel knew Ben was annoyed.

The reached the lightkeeper's cottage and stopped at the front steps. He picked a blade of grass and tossed it to the wind. His face was all hard planes.

"I was leaving because I wanted to protect you."

"I don't need protection, Rachel." Frustration punctuated his words.

"So Ida told me."

He tilted his head back. His gray eyes took in every detail of her face. "Is that the only reason?"

She remembered his kiss. "Of course."

His eyes narrowed a fraction. "You are a bad liar, Rachel."

She blinked, shocked by his candor.

"You left because of the kiss."

She hugged her bundle close to her chest as if it were a shield over her heart. "I shouldn't have kissed you."

Rachel dropped her gaze. She wasn't a virgin. There'd been Peter, of course, but the sex between them had been cold and unsatisfying. After her initial fears of the bedroom had passed, Peter had lost interest in her sexually. He'd not come to her room in over eight months.

She'd been kissed by suitors when she'd made her debut, but no man's touch had rocked her as Ben's kiss had. She'd felt it in every sinew of her body.

Still to talk about such desires out loud felt wanton. "The kiss scared me."

Ben's hand tilted her head up so she looked at him. "Was it distasteful?"

Heat rushed through her body. "It was quite pleasant. Too pleasant."

"You ran because you liked it."

"Yes."

A hint of a smile borne of masculine pride touched his lips. "There is something between us, Rachel. I've felt it and so have you."

"That's the problem." She spoke so softly.

He released her chin and traced his knuckle along her jawline. "Why?"

"Perhaps because I am half starved for affection. I've had none in so long. I fear I will drink up whatever you offer. And when I am satisfied, I won't want you anymore."

He took her hand in his. "You are honest. That I appreciate."

Honest. She'd not been honest with him. She was a liar and a fraud in so many ways.

Gently he traced circles on her palm with his callused thumb. "What if I'm willing to take the chance on us?"

She couldn't think when he touched her. "I am damaged goods, Ben. I am good to no man anymore."

His jaw hardened. "You are afraid, but you are not damaged, Rachel. You are a young, vital woman."

Tears filled her eyes. "I feel as if I am one hundred years old." She tipped her head back. When she'd stemmed the tide of tears, she met his gaze again.

"This is about your husband."

"What?" She could barely breath. "H-he's dead."

"The marriage was bad."

"Yes."

"But it is over now."

"Yes! I will never go back to my old life."

He nodded. "As I've said, this is a good place to start over."

"Is that why you came back after you left the Navy?"

"Yes."

"What happened?"

He shoved out a breath. "Six months had passed since the peace treaty in Appomattox had been signed. Though most of the field commanders knew of the surrender, some of the Confederate sea captains did not." He straightened his shoulders. "I was in command of a warship bound for England with a load of delegates—both American and British. The whole trip was designed to show the Brits we were a united country again, the war was over. We were in the North Atlantic when we spotted a ship on the horizon. It was the *C.S.S. Alabama.* I knew her commander was a shrewd man and a great fighter. I'd heard he'd not surrendered. An American delegate aboard—Mr. Martin—ordered that we approach the *Alabama.* I didn't want to, knowing the risks. However, Mr. Martin insisted. I'd been told before we left port to obey his orders.

"I alerted my first officer to ready the guns and then we turned about to an intercept course. As we approached the *Alabama,* she fired on us. I didn't hesitate to fire back. The lives of my men and passengers were at stake and I wasn't going to stand by and let my ship go down. We chased off the *Alabama,* but the incident infuriated Mr. Martin. He'd been humiliated in front of the Brits. He filed charges when we hit port." Ben shrugged. "I was court-martialed."

"That wasn't fair."

"Who ever said life was supposed to be fair?"

She suspected he underplayed his feelings. He wasn't the kind of man who swallowed injustice well. "The time had come for me to leave, anyway. I'd done all I could do in the Navy. They didn't need warriors anymore. They needed diplomats. I'm not known for my subtlety."

So she'd noticed. "You are not sorry you were forced to leave?"

"I am home now. This is where I belong."

They stood inches apart in silence for several minutes. A flock of seagulls flew overhead, squawking as they circled. The wind rustled the sea oats on the dunes. The tang of the ocean hung in the air.

He rubbed his thumb over her knuckles. Standing here with him, she didn't feel lost. She felt as if she could conquer any obstacle.

Ben was so close, all she had to do was to lean forward and her lips would touch his. Desire, not fear, drove her this time. She craved the taste of him; wanted to feel his arms wrapped around her again.

"I'm finished running," she said.

He squeezed her hand. "Good."

Rachel spent a restless day and night. Ben had been on duty and she'd tossed and turned, unable to fall into a deep sleep.

She'd dreamed of teaching the children. Of living here on the outer banks with Ben. And of monsters....

At dawn she had awoken, unable to spend another hour in bed. She'd made tea and sliced a piece of day-old bread. Once she'd cleaned up, there was nothing to do. She looked around the lightkeeper's cottage, peeking into closets and closed-off rooms.

She perused Ben's collection of books, still in crates in the parlor. She even found a couple of books that held interest. She curled up on the sofa in front of the fire and opened a book.

She read the first line. Her attention wandered and she skipped to the next paragraph. Before she realized it, she'd leafed through fifty or so pages without having read a word.

Frustrated, Rachel closed the book and rose. She paced the parlor. Her restlessness grew and she found the walls of the cottage starting to shrink around her.

She had to get out.

Fear wasn't motivating her as she grabbed her coat. Annoyance was.

She had the freedom to choose, to live her life now as she pleased and yet she stayed hidden in this cottage.

She shoved her arms into the sleeves of her coat. "I'm not going to keep doing this to myself. I need to live my life."

Rachel went outside. She'd go to the village and be among people. She wasn't sure what she intended to do once she got to town. There'd been a time when she'd been completely at ease with strangers; she could walk into a room and strike up a conversation with anyone. But in the last year, she'd fallen out of practice. She'd all but forgotten how to talk to people.

She enjoyed the walk into the village. The cold breeze flapped her skirts as she savored the crisp air and azure sky. This was a fickle land. Already she'd learned that the weather changed without warning here.

The sound of children laughing trickled through the tall thicket of bushes aligning the path. Rachel stopped, smiling.

"Johnny is *it!*" cried a young girl. "Johnny, you must count to ten while we hide now!"

Johnny mumbled something about cheaters, but soon she could hear him counting, "One, two…"

Peals of laughter mingled with the thud of feet against the sandy earth. "Don't peek," a girl shouted.

"You always peek, Johnny Freely," another girl squealed.

Rachel started to move silently down the path, not wanting to disturb their game. Just hearing them bolstered her spirits.

She came to the edge of the pathway, which opened onto a small clearing dotted by shrubs. A wind-bent tree stood in the center of the field. There she saw a young boy, not more than seven. He had red hair, a worn shirt, and jacket and pants that were two inches too short. He had dirty hands over his eyes and he peeked between his index and pinky fingers. He counted, "Seven, eight…

Rachel smiled. "I thought you weren't supposed to look, Johnny."

Startled, the boy dropped his hands and stared up her as if she had three heads. "How do you know my name?"

She stood still, worried that she'd frighten him more. "I heard the girls calling to you. They said you always peek."

He frowned. "I don't always peek."

"You were this time."

He scrunched up his nose. "That's because the girls have made me 'it' seven times in a row. I'm sick of being 'it.'"

"Cheating isn't the way."

He walked toward her, his hands in his pockets. "I wasn't cheating exactly. It's not like I could see anything."

"But you were trying."

He shrugged. "Lot of good it did me."

Rachel liked the boy.

A little girl about the age of ten with blond braids and a calico dress poked her head out from behind a tree. "Hey, Johnny, are you going to come and find us or not?"

When the girl spotted Rachel, her gaze narrowed. She called, "Emma!" Instantly another girl of about the same age popped up from behind a shrub.

The girls approached Rachel. Their gazes narrowed; they were clearly leery of her.

"Who's this?" the first girl said to Johnny.

"How am I supposed to know?"

Rachel clasped her hands in front of her. "My name is Rachel. What are your names?"

The first girl said, "I'm Ruth and this is my sister Emma and our cousin Johnny."

"It's a pleasure to meet you."

"Are you the shipwrecked lady?" Emma asked.

Rachel nodded. "I am."

Ruth studied Rachel. "Billy Michaels said you are a mermaid."

Laughing, Rachel raised her skirts a fraction to show her feet and ankles. "I'm afraid not. Just very lucky Mr. Mitchell was there to save me."

Johnny rubbed his nose. "He saves a lot of people."

"How did you get that black eye?" Rachel asked.

He shrugged. "Some mainland kid at the school. He didn't like my clothes. I punched him. He punched me back." He looked at her. "Ma said you had a bruised eye."

Instinctively she touched her left eye. "I did."

He studied her. "Who hit you?"

"A bad man," Rachel said. "I don't plan on seeing him ever again."

"I wish I didn't have to see those dumb boys again," Johnny said.

Emma looked up at Rachel, her eyes wise beyond her years. "The mainland children don't like us too much. They make fun of our clothes and the way we talk."

Ruth scowled. "They're creeps."

Rachel's heart opened to the children. "Ida tells me you have to go back on Sunday."

Johnny kicked the sand. "I ain't going back. I've had it with the mainland. I'd rather be dumb as dirt than go back."

"He always says that," said Ruth. "But Uncle Horace always puts him on the boat."

"Ruth, Johnny, Emma!" The woman's voice drifted through the trees.

"That's Ma," said Emma. "We've got to go."

Without another word, the children ran down the path and disappeared around the bend.

Rachel stood silent. She'd lost her desire to wander around the village. She knew what she wanted to do now.

Captain LaFortune sat by the candle in the old fisherman's shack. In his hand he held the ring the woman had given him. The rubies glistened in the light.

Forever and always.

The words meant nothing to him. Foolish sentiment. The tossed the ring up in the air and caught it in his hand.

He could trade the ring in town for just about anything he wanted, but he sensed it was worth far more.

LaFortune held it close to the candle and studied the intricate engraving on the inside. That's when he saw the initials. R.E.

They were the initials of the woman!

Excited, he turned the ring over and over in his hand. Who was she?

He knew if he could figure out R.E.'s identity, he could recapture his fortune.

R.E.

She'd had blond hair, vivid blue eyes and soft white skin. And of course the dark bruise that had marred her skin.

To damage such beauty was a sin. He'd take a woman like R.E. to bed; he'd never beat her.

He shoved out a sigh. But there were men in this world that took more enjoyment from the pain than the pleasure.

R.E.

So young. So lovely.

He'd seen her before but where? And her smoky voice had stoked memories he couldn't quite bring into focus.

LaFortune let his mind drift to the ports he'd sailed this last year. New York. Baltimore. Washington.

The answer danced at the edges of his mind just out of reach. R.E.

E for Edgar, Eggleston, Edmondson. Emmons.

Peter Emmons! Rachel Emmons!

The answer came to him in a flash. He clutched the ring in his hands and laughed out loud. *"Bien!"*

He'd met Peter Emmons and his lovely wife Rachel in New York this past spring. He'd been taken by the woman's beauty but he'd quickly realized Peter didn't like any man looking too closely at his wife. The man had been obsessed with his Rachel.

Rachel's bruise, her widow's weeds and her impatience to leave all made sense now. She'd run away from her husband.

LaFortune smiled.

Emmons was a rich man, indeed.

And no doubt he'd pay a small fortune to get his runaway wife back.

Chapter Twelve

Excitement had Rachel walking briskly toward Ida's shop. Teaching the children would be the perfect job for her. For the first time in a long while, she had something to look forward to.

The bells on the door jingled as she walked inside. The aroma of spices and herbs greeted her. Ida stood by the bolts of fabric next to Callie.

"Callie, you need to stop fretting about all the details. You are going to be a lovely bride." Ida glanced up at the door. "Rachel, it's good to see you. Come in."

Callie glanced quickly at Rachel. "Hi, Rachel."

Rachel smiled. "Hello."

Callie turned her attention back to the lace. She chewed her bottom lip. "I just want everything to be perfect. And this lace Sara made for the dress looks awful. I can't wear it on my wedding day."

"I'm not telling Sara her needlework isn't what it used to be." Ida looked up at Rachel. "Thank heavens, another woman to talk sense into this jittery bride."

Rachel moved toward them, unsure if she should give advice to any young bride-to-be.

Callie held up the lace collar. Her eyes were red. "Look at this collar and tell me it's beautiful."

Rachel took the hand-made lace collar. Crooked, with dozens of missed stitches, it looked a mess. Still, someone had put time into it. "Who made this?"

"Sara Crocket," Ida supplied.

"She's old and very spry," Rachel said. She remembered how the old woman's eyes had softened when she'd spoken to Ben. "And I suspect she loves you very much."

"She's a dear," Callie said.

"Then I would wear the collar," Rachel said. "Sara's love is in this piece, making it far more lovely than expert stitching."

"See, Callie?" Ida said. "Sara spent five days working on that collar for you. She wanted to make your dress special. She made the lace for my dress when I married my second husband."

"I thought the collar would be beautiful," Callie said. Her eyes started to tear.

"Sara used to make the loveliest lace. But her eyes have started to fail," Ida said.

"I just want to be perfect for Timothy," Callie said. "And that collar looks so awful. But I can't tell Sara that. It'll hurt her feelings. And I don't know the first thing about lacework."

The girl's dramatics had Ida shaking her head and Rachel remembering a time when she'd been just as passionate about the silliest things. She also understood there'd be no reasoning with Callie over the lace. "If you've a lace hook, I could fix it for you."

Callie's eyes brightened. "The wedding is tomorrow."

"I'm handy with a needlework and lace hooks." It was one of the few activities Peter had approved of. She'd spent hours by the fire making samplers and lace dollies that in the end were stored away.

"There isn't any time," Callie said.

Rachel fingered the lace. "It won't take me any time at all."

Ida shook her head. "It would hurt Sara to know that you redid her collar, Callie."

Callie's eyes widened. "I won't tell!"

"And I can reproduce what she's done here,"

Rachel said. "I recognize the pattern. It can do it this afternoon."

Callie squeezed Rachel's hands. "You are wonderful. And tell me you are coming to the wedding with Ben."

"Ben hasn't said anything about us coming together," Rachel said.

"Just like a man," Ida remarked.

"Well, he wasn't sure if I planned to stay," Rachel added.

Ida nodded. "And you are now?"

"Yes," Rachel said.

Ida smiled. "I wouldn't fret over it. He'll get around to asking. Men aren't good with social details."

"And Ben's the worst," Callie said. "He's giving me away so he has to be there. And we'd love to have you."

"I don't want to impose on your day," Rachel said.

Callie took her hands in hers. "You are saving my *life* by redoing that collar," she said. "I can think of no one else I'd like to have there."

Rachel smiled. "I will take care of the collar."

Callie pulled a lace hook and a ball of extra thread from her pocket. "Thank you!"

Ida handed Callie a basketful of flour sacks and

spices. "Get on back to your mother-in-law's. She'll be needing that flour if she's going to make your cake."

The young woman beamed and headed out the door. Ida shook her head, turning to a pile of material in need of folding. "That girl runs me ragged. I hope Timothy knows what he's getting into."

"Does anyone when they marry?"

Ida laughed. "No."

Rachel began to fold a piece of fabric. "I was thinking about the children in town and the fact that they have to travel so far for school."

"Pity, isn't it."

Nervous energy shot through Rachel. "Have you considered opening a school on the island?"

"We've all talked about it enough, but like I said before, there's no teacher."

"I could teach."

Ida stopped and looked at her. "You?"

Rachel feared if she didn't keep talking she'd lose her nerve. "I've no experience directly with teaching, but I've been to many excellent schools. I love to read and I enjoy children. It could be a perfect fit for everyone."

"You take a job like that, you just can't pick up and leave. You'll have to commit yourself to this place."

"I know. Honestly, I think that I could love this place."

Before Ida could answer, the bells on the front door jingled. "Don't look now," Ida said, smiling brightly. "You're about to be baptized by fire."

Three women from the village entered. Their dark dresses and gray bonnets made them look as tired and weather-beaten as the town.

A short woman stepped forward. Her hips were round and her eyes small like raisins. Her gaze darted to Rachel. She frowned. "Ida, we came by to see what else needs doing for the wedding."

Ida grabbed a jar of peppermints. "There is so much to do by tomorrow and I'm so far behind." She opened the jar. "Would you like a candy?"

The short woman took a candy. "Mighty generous of you, Ida."

Ida passed the jar from woman to woman. "Before we talk about the wedding, there is something else I wanted to bring up."

Rachel sucked in a deep breath.

Ida's clear and steady voice calmed her. "Have you all met Rachel? She's the gal Ben pulled from the ocean."

The women studied Rachel. They nodded but none spoke. The stocky woman pulled in her stomach a fraction.

"Rachel, these three ladies are the cornerstones of this town. Don't know what I'd do without them. This here is Marianne Freely, her husband is Horace." Mrs. Freely nodded, straightening her shoulders a fraction as she eyed Rachel.

Ida pointed to a woman with large bosoms and ink-black hair. "This is Ella Harter and next to her," she said, pointing to a very slim woman with auburn hair, "this is Sylvia Winters."

"It's a pleasure, ladies," Rachel said.

The women murmured their greeting but clearly they were suspicious of Rachel.

Ida set the jar down. "Remember how we were talking after church a while back about starting a school on the island?"

Mrs. Freely reached for another candy. "A good idea but impossible."

Ida held up her finger. "Maybe not. I've an idea that Rachel Davis could start a school for the children here in the village."

Shocked whispers rose among the women.

Rachel stood straight, aware that all the women's gazes bore into her now.

"Think about it," Ida said. "We'd talked about converting a boathouse or even the base of the lighthouse into a schoolroom. Now that we have Rachel interested in teaching, we can have our school. We'd no longer be at the mercy of the rising prices of the boarding school. We'd no longer have to worry over the weather when our children cross to the mainland."

"But our children are getting a good education on the mainland," Mrs. Harter said. "We know nothing about this woman, except that Ben pulled her out of the water and she's been living with him."

Ida planted her hands on her hips. Her silver hair glistened in the morning sun. "Ella, I can tell you she's smart. Comes from quality. She can give the children more than that dried-up prune at Webster's school."

"And who's to say she's gonna stay," Mrs. Freely said. "Be nothing worse than to cancel our spots at Webster's and then have her leave."

Rachel smoothed damp hands over her skirt. "Ida, if I might address the ladies."

Everyone turned to face her. No one was smiling.

A shiver of apprehension danced down her spine. She'd never felt more out of place. The tension in the room was thick.

"I am well versed in reading and writing as well as French and Latin."

"You ever teach?" Sylvia asked.

Rachel faced the woman, meeting her direct

gaze. "No. But I've been educated in schools in London, Paris and New York. I've read more books than I can remember and I know I'd love working with the children."

Mrs. Harter stepped forward. "I have a thirteen-year-old and a five-year-old. You gonna teach both of them in the same classroom? My daughter is smart as a whip and has been reading since she was five but my boy only wants to fish. The teachers spend half the time dragging him back to his seat."

"There will be challenges for all of us," Rachel said.

Mrs. Winters shook her head. "I don't like the idea of the children crossing. Makes my blood run cold. But my girl is having trouble reading. Says the words are backward. If I put her in your school, could you fix that?"

Rachel didn't know. "I'd need time to evaluate her."

Mrs. Winters frowned, clearly not happy with the answer.

"Let's not mince words," Mrs. Freely said. "We don't know this woman. She washed up on our shores and all we know about her is that Ben likes her. Now, I ain't doubting that she's smart, that she *might* be a decent teacher one day, but I ain't pulling my children from school unless I know she's staying."

"I give you my word that I will stay a year," Rachel said.

"Ain't enough," Mrs. Harter said. "We don't know you well enough to know that you'll keep your word."

Mrs. Freely nodded. "And, frankly, I'm not keen on the idea of you living so free and easy with the lightkeeper. That kind of domestic relationship is hard to explain to a child."

"I can assure you that my relationship with Mr. Mitchell is quite respectable," Rachel said.

"Might be now," Mrs. Harter said. "But we don't know that it'll stay that way."

Ida frowned. "My Ben's an honorable man."

"Aye, he is," Mrs. Winters said. "But he is a man and having a woman like Rachel Davis under his roof would test the patience of a saint."

Mrs. Freely's lips flattened. "Ida, I say we call a vote. I for one don't think the idea of this woman teaching our children is a good one."

Rachel could feel the ground under her feet eroding like the sand on the beach. "Is there anything that I can say to change your mind?"

More murmurs followed. "No," Mrs. Freely said. "Let's get to the vote. I've got my morning catch to clean. All those in favor of Rachel Davis teaching our children, say aye."

The room was quiet.

Ida stepped forward. "Aye."

Rachel's stomach clenched. She managed a smile for Ida.

"All those opposed."

A resounding "Nay" reverberated off the walls.

Rachel's heart sank.

Rachel didn't see Ben all afternoon. She'd half expected him to come by the cottage but his work had kept him very busy. She'd dearly have loved to tell him about what had happened in the village that day. But he never came.

She retreated to the parlor and spent the afternoon sitting by the fire remaking the lace collar for Callie. When the sun went down, she turned up the lanterns and continued to work the white tread into lace.

As she pulled the treads loose, she remembered her own wedding dress, a watered silk by Worth. It had cost a fortune partly because Peter had wanted it made and delivered within three weeks. Every detail of their marriage had been rushed. He'd paid a king's ransom for the reception. At the time, she'd thought he'd loved her, now she realized that it was his need to possess that drove him.

A clock on the mantel ticked. Her wedding day had been only a year ago, it was but a vague memory now. The yards of silk, the vases of flowers and the elegant meal had faded to the shadows—almost as if it had never happened. *Almost.*

The clock on the mantel chimed twelve times. She'd finished the collar and with the extra thread made two cuffs. Together with the collar, she draped them over a chair for safekeeping. Ben usually came home for dinner before his shift, but not tonight.

Rachel picked up her lantern and moved into the kitchen. She knelt in front of the stove, opened the small door at the bottom and shoved in pieces of kindling. The red embers sparked and popped. Satisfied, she closed the door and rose. She pulled the kettle onto the front burner.

She moved into the pantry and found the ham she'd seen earlier. With a large kitchen blade, she took the ham to the table. The knife felt unwieldy and awkward in her hand. She hacked away a small, uneven piece.

Rachel dug the knife in deeper as footsteps sounded on the back porch. Startled, the blade slipped through the meat quickly and cut directly into her hand.

She dropped the knife and looked at her hand. Blood oozed from her index finger.

Ben strode into the room as she turned and headed to the sink to wipe the cut off. "What are you still doing up?" he said, moving toward her.

She felt foolish for cutting herself. "I was hungry and wanted a snack." She reached for the pitcher of water.

"Have you cut yourself?" he said.

Holding the full water pitcher with one hand while keeping her bleeding finger over the sink was awkward. "Yes. A stupid accident." She curled her injured hand into a fist, as if to hide her blunder.

He approached her with the lantern. He took her injured hand in his and inspected the wound. The cold night air still clung to him and he smelled of fresh air and the barest hint of oil.

His hands were rough, deeply callused, as he uncurled her fingers. "I just sharpened that blade a few days ago. You're lucky you didn't cut your finger off."

"Who'd have thought a simple task would turn into such trouble? Agnes always made it look so easy when she carved."

He reached for the pitcher and poured the cool water over the cut. "Agnes?"

She hissed in a breath. "Our cook."

"Our?" he said, never lifting his gaze from her hand.

Rachel shifted and tried to pull her hand free. "My father had a cook." Another half-truth. Another lie by omission.

Ben held tight. "You've never talked about your father."

"He died more than a year ago."

"I'm sorry to hear that." He reached for a dry dishcloth and wrapped it around her hand. He covered her injured hand with his. His touch sent heat leaping through her. "You won't need a stitch. Just keep this wrapped around your hand tonight and it should seal itself."

Lantern light flickered on his face. "Thank you."

His dark gaze bore into her. "So you've been on your own this past year?"

"No." She pulled away from him, reasoning somehow if he couldn't see her face he wouldn't see the truth she so desperately wanted to forget. She tensed, ready for more questions, but they never came.

Drying his hands, he moved to the kitchen table and picked up the knife. "You're hungry?"

"Yes," she said, grateful.

He sliced the knife into the meat with ease.

Soon four thick pieces lay stacked on the cutting board. "Then sit and I'll make us plates."

She sat. "You're always feeding me."

He shrugged. "You're still too thin." He laid a plate of sliced ham on the table.

"How was your shift tonight?"

"Not busy. No sign of ships."

"That's good."

He moved to the cupboard and pulled down two mugs. He touched the side of the kettle to test the heat. "The water's not quite ready."

"I only just moved it onto the heat."

He put bread on the table. "What were you doing up so late tonight?"

This quiet moment seemed so normal. "I was making a lace collar and cuffs for Callie's wedding dress."

He lifted an eyebrow. "Really?"

"Seems Sara had tried to make a collar but Callie wasn't pleased."

He grunted. "Callie can be a bit choosy at times."

Rachel shrugged. "It's good for a girl to know what she wants. I certainly didn't at her age." She hesitated. "Callie invited me to her wedding."

Ben nodded. "I'd meant to ask you but with all the work today I forgot."

It piqued her pride that he'd forgotten her today. She doubted he worried over social niceties too much. "I see."

"I will need to work in the morning before the service." Lantern light flickered on his stoic face. "But I'd be pleased to meet you at the church. We can sit together."

His simple invitation had her blushing. "Yes."

Ben smiled. "Then it's a date."

Chapter Thirteen

Warm days in March were rare this close to the water. Add to the fact that the children were home and there was a wedding today, it made sense that the village buzzed with excitement.

Rachel, with the lace cuffs and collar wrapped in a clean cloth, walked down the center street toward the church, a small, white, rectangular building with a simple cross atop a spire. Fiddle music mingled with the sound of laughter.

A crowd of villagers gathered by the front door of the church. The women reminisced about their wedding days. The men talked of younger days when their lives were simpler and full of possibilities.

Rachel sidestepped the crowds by the front door of the church and went directly to the back. She climbed the three small steps and entered through a door that led to a small room behind the altar. There she found Callie and Ida.

The room was simple, furnished only with two chairs and a small table pushed against the wall. A wooden cross hung on the wall. On the table lay a bouquet of wild flowers tied together with a yellow ribbon.

Ida wore a light blue wool dress. She'd brushed her silver-gray hair up and pinned it under a smart derby-style hat. She'd fastened a sprig of sea oats tied with a white ribbon on her right shoulder.

Callie wore a pale yellow dress. Her auburn hair hung down and atop her head sat a ring of flowers. Flushed cheeks accentuated eyes bright with nervous excitement.

"You've made it," Callie said.

"I was starting to worry," Ida said.

"I slept a bit late this morning," Rachel said. After she'd made her date with Ben last night, she'd been in knots. Unreasonably excited, she'd tossed and turned, unable to sleep.

"Do you have the collar?" Callie said.

"And cuffs to match." Rachel unfolded the fabric and held the up for Callie.

The young woman rushed toward her. Tears filled her eyes as she reverently studied the intricate work. "Oh, my, they are stunning."

Ida studied Rachel's handiwork. "You are an artist, Rachel."

Pride swelled in her. "I wanted it to be just right."

"I've never seen lace more fine. You must have been up half the night."

All night, thanks to Ben. "Let me stitch it to your dress."

Ida pulled a small ladder-backed chair from the wall and set it in the middle of the tiny room. Callie sat and held up her hair.

"This is so kind of you," Callie said.

"Aye," Ida agreed. "The lace will make the day all the more special."

Rachel laid the lace over the collar. She pulled a small needle and thread that she'd pinned earlier to the cloth. "It fits perfectly."

Callie nodded. "This whole day is perfect."

"I saw Timothy," Ida said. "He looks fine in his dark coat."

Callie's eyes beamed. "He is a handsome man."

"Did Ben come with you?"

"He'll be here soon. There were a few last-minute details to attend to at the lighthouse."

Ida nodded knowing. "There always are. But knowing my Ben, he'll be here."

"He's giving me away," Callie said, her voice full of excitement.

Rachel began to stitch the lace to the collar. This is how a bride-to-be should look and feel on her wedding day—excited and radiant. The day she'd been married, she'd been alone as she'd waited in the small room off the sanctuary. She'd held her bouquet of white roses, longing for her mother and wondering when the day would come when she'd look at her husband and feel love. The day had never come.

Organ music in the church began. The rich notes filled the building. Rachel's throat tightened with emotion.

Ida squeezed her niece's hand. "This is it. Ben should be waiting for you at the back of the church."

Rachel handed Callie her bouquet. She arranged ribbon streamers so that they cascaded neatly. "You look lovely."

Ida eyes widened. "Have you got everything you should have? Something old?"

Callie touched a small crucifix hanging around her neck. "My necklace from Grandmother Betty."

"Something borrowed and something blue?"

Callie produced a blue handkerchief from her cousin. "It's borrowed and blue."

"And something new?"

The young bride-to-be touched her collar. "The lace."

There'd never been anyone to ask these questions of Rachel. "You are ready to go."

"I am," Callie said with a confidence borne of love.

The next half hour sped by. Rachel took the place next to Ida. The tall windows flanking each side of the long narrow room were adorned with sprigs of sea oats and candles. On a table behind the altar, wildflowers filled a silver vase. The church was simple, some from her old life would say primitive, yet she'd never seen anything more beautiful.

The organist stopped. Timothy came out the side door with his brother and stood at the front of the church with the minister. The minister nodded to the organist and she started to play louder.

Rachel turned with everyone else and saw Callie and Ben standing at the back of the church. Callie stared up at him, adoration in her eyes. She looked stunning.

Ben wore dark blue pants and a double-breasted jacket with brass buttons. He'd shaven and brushed back his hair, which curled just above the collar of his black turtleneck. Rachel's heart tripped. She'd never seen a more handsome man.

A wave of ahs swept across the room as Ben placed Callie's arm on his and walked her down the isle. Timothy, standing tall, grinned with pride as his young bride moved up the aisle. Ben placed Callie's hand in Timothy's and stepped back. He sat next to Rachel on the pew.

His shoulder brushed hers as he scooted closer. He looked down at her and winked. She nearly melted into the seat.

Rachel dragged her gaze from his to Callie and Timothy.

The young couple held hands and faced each other as the other couple repeated their vows. "Do you Timothy take Callie to be your wedded wife?" The minister's voice echoed in the small church.

"I do." Timothy's answer was strong.

"Callie, do you take Timothy to be your lawful husband?"

Callie beamed. "I sure do!"

Everyone laughed. The young girl exuded so much joy and excitement.

When the minister pronounced them married, Ben reached down and squeezed Rachel's hand.

She looked up into his smiling eyes. Instead of happiness, an overwhelming loneliness overtook her. She could never stand before a minister and pledge her life to Ben.

And the thought broke her heart.

* * *

The reception was held in a large boathouse at the end of town. The dories in for repair had been moved out, and sawhorses and wood planks had been set up and covered with an assortment of table clothes. An assortment of hams, vegetables, freshly backed pies, breads and cakes filled the table.

Women milled around the food table happily swapping gossip and stories of recent births. The men had tapped a keg of whiskey next to a fiddle player who'd struck up a tune. Rachel spotted Johnny chasing Emma and Ruth with a worm.

As she peered into the building, Rachel saw that Ben stood in a receiving line with Ida, Timothy and Callie. He glanced up at her and winked. Her heart melted.

She'd dearly have loved to spend time with him but it was clear he'd not be free of well-wishers for a while.

On her own, she felt awkward. She saw Mrs. Freely, Harter and Winters taking in a corner by the fiddle players. Mrs. Harter glanced up, saw Rachel, but made no move to welcome her. She turned her back as if she'd not seen her.

Drawing in a breath, Rachel moved into the crowed room and stood next to the table. She traced circles with her finger on the tablecloth as the smells, the music, the laughter swirled around her head.

She caught the eye of several women. She smiled. The women looked away. The men openly watched her, but none approached.

Rachel hugged her shawl around her. She was very aware that she was an outsider.

Drawing in a breath, Rachel walked up to a woman standing alone next to a half-eaten carrot cake on the table.

Rachel made herself smile. "The cake looks lovely."

The woman, not much older than she, looked up with brown eyes filled with concern. "Do you think so? It's half eaten. My brothers ate half while I was doing the wash yesterday. I was so mad, but I had no time to bake another."

"It looks so delicious. I bet no one will worry how many slices have been cut once they taste it."

The woman smiled. "Do you think so?"

"I know so."

"My name is Hanna Winters. And you are Rachel."

Rachel accepted Hanna's hand. Calluses rubbed against her smooth palm. "Everyone knows me."

"Not often Ben fishes a woman from the sea."

"Hopefully, I won't need to be fished out again. Once was quite enough."

Hanna laughed. "Ah, the water is lovely to look at but we've all a healthy respect for it. Everyone here has lost someone to the sea."

"Have you lost any one?" The question was out before Rachel realized it. "I'm sorry, that's a rude question."

Hanna shrugged. "Not rude at all." She hesitated. "I lost my husband last year in a gale. It tipped his fishing boat and he drowned."

"I'm sorry."

"I've managed. My mother-in-law has not fared so well."

Rachel pictured the somber woman with the stern, lined face. "I've met Sylvia Winters."

Her heart went out to Mrs. Winters. The pain of losing a child, even one fully grown, must be devastating.

Before she could think what to say, the fiddle music started up. Hanna, seeming to shake off her melancholy, started clapping in tune with the music.

Soon men and women started pairing up and moving to the center of the room. Women lined up on one side, the men the other and soon all were dancing a Virginia reel.

Rachel started to tap her foot and soon she was clapping in time with the music.

"Sloan plays the best fiddle in five counties."

Rachel watched the man pick at the strings as he sat on a crate. With a pint of ale at his feet, he laughed as several people around him started to sing.

Their good humor was infectious. Rachel clapped her hands in time with the music.

Two young men walked up to Hanna asked for a dance. One was as tall as a bean pole the other short and muscular.

The shorter one smiled at Hanna. "Like to take a spin?"

Hanna beamed. "I'd love to, Fred." She accepted his hand.

Fred drew Hanna close. "Maybe your friend would like to dance with Steve."

Hanna absently leaned into Fred. "Rachel? What do you say?"

Panic hit Rachel. She glanced up at Steve. At least two decades older, his full cheeks suggested he'd never missed a meal and his small back eyes reminded her of coat.

He held out his hand. "Ma'am?"

What could a dance hurt? Certainly, Ben wouldn't mind. Besides, Rachel as doing what she'd wanted to do for months. She was living.

Rachel took his hand. It was cold, damp with sweat. Steve guided her out to the floor they each stood in a line facing each other. Before she realized it, he'd spun her around. She fell into the steps easily.

The line shifted and she faced another man. This gentleman looked to be in his seventies, but he had a spry step.

Soon she was laughing, easily shifting down the row to another new partner. Time sped by.

She looked up and spotted Ben across the room. He was dancing with a buxom woman with red curls. She had a loud boisterous laugh and she clearly liked dancing with Ben. Several times she leaned forward, touching her breasts to his chest, to whisper something in Ben's ear.

Rachel missed a step. Suddenly, she didn't feel like dancing.

To her surprise, she was jealous.

Rachel was having her third cup of punch, which was very good indeed—so fruity. The sun had set and the air cooled, but she felt excessively warm and a bit lightheaded.

She'd lost sight of Ben and the big-breasted redhead more than an hour ago, and she found herself feeling a bit put out. It wasn't any of her business who he spent his time with. He'd made no promises to her and she certainly couldn't make any. But that didn't cool the jealousy humming in her veins.

"So you've finally stopped dancing." Ben's deep voice sounded just behind her.

Pride had her turning slowly. His shoulders back, his well-worn boots ate the distance between them.

The noise around her faded. A potent, heavy desire hummed in her veins. His gaze bore into her. Heat rose in her cheeks.

Two children ran in front of Ben, forcing him to halt his advance. He stopped, tall, proud, smiling ruefully as they ran past him.

Rachel's stomach fluttered. He closed the distance between them.

"I wasn't sure if I'd ever get to see you tonight."

"I had to return to the lighthouse and light the lanterns."

"You spent a good deal of time with a redhead, I noticed."

He grinned. "Why, Rachel, are you jealous?"

She lifted her chin. "Not a bit. It was just hard not to notice her.

"I've known Molly for years."

How well? she wondered churlishly. "I'm sure she's a lovely woman."

Laughing, Ben took her punch cup from her. "How many of those have you had?"

"Three."

He set the cup on a table and cupped her elbow in his hand. "From what I hear they mixed the wine from the *Anna St. Claire* with cider."

Rachel giggled. "Do you know that wine cost twenty dollars a bottle?"

"Whatever the cost it's a hit." He touched her nose with the tip of his finger. "And you're looped."

Wind and sea mingled with his masculine scent. An invisible force pulled her toward him. She'd enjoyed dancing with the other men, but she'd not felt the pull she felt for Ben.

She lifted her chin. "I'm perfectly fine."

"Let's walk."

She didn't argue. The air in the room had grown stifling.

"It looks like it's a grand party," he said. She sensed he could care less about the party.

"Callie is beautiful. Timothy is prouder than a peacock. I've had a wonderful time." She stumbled.

He caught her and pulled her against his side. "Careful."

His masculine presence enveloped her. Her breathing grew shallow. Her heart hammered in her chest. The music and laughter of the party seemed quite distant now.

She looked up into his gray eyes. Lord, but she wanted to kiss him.

Steve followed them outside. "Let's dance, Rachel."

He smelled of whiskey and swayed ever so slightly. However, she didn't want to be rude. He'd been kind this evening.

Ben didn't share her reservations. "Rachel and I were just going for a walk."

"Ah, let me have one more dance with her. Ben, have a drink while we dance," Steve said. He took Rachel by the arm.

Ben clamped his hand on Steve's shoulder. "Another time."

Slowly, Steve uncurled his fingers from Rachel's arm. His gaze hardened and he didn't step back. "Another dance later, Rachel?"

"Perhaps," she said. His shift in mood frightened her.

"I'm going to hold you to a dance, Rachel," Steve said.

Gently, Ben cupped her elbow, a clear show of possession. "Much, much later."

Ben guided Rachel further away from the party.

They left Steve behind standing alone by the door table his left hand fisted.

"He's not very happy," Rachel said.

"He'll survive."

They stepped outside. A thousand stars winked in the clear, night air. In the distance seagulls squawked.

Ben wrapped his long fingers wrapped around her hand. She was surprised how well their hands fit together. They walked along the main street. The light from the boat barn glowed behind them. If this were a perfect world, she and Ben would be courting, perhaps dreaming of a wedding day like today.

"I only have an hour before I must get back at check the lanterns."

"Do you ever get tired of working in the lighthouse?"

"I thought maybe I would at first. But I've discovered this place is in my bones."

"I admire your conviction," Rachel said. Her head barely reached his shoulders.

He stopped laid his hands on her shoulders. Moonlight reflected off his blue-black hair. He touched curled end of her hair.

He stood so close to her. She stared at the curve of his lips and wondered if they tasted as salty and sweet as they had before. His lips covered hers.

She felt the tension in his. She parted her lips, ready for him to kiss her.

"I've been thinking about us."

The sound of his voice broke the spell. She realized with utter embarrassment that she'd been staring at his lips.

Rachel's breath caught in her throat. Lord, but she feared he was going to bring up talk of marriage. "Ben."

"I heard what happened in the store yesterday."

Relief and disappointment collided. "I've tried not to think about it or what I'm going to do to support herself. My money won't last forever and I'll go mad just pacing the cottage."

"You could have given up. You didn't. I admire that."

"Your stubbornness is wearing off on me."

"I have a job offer."

"What?"

"The rescue service will be visiting the island the first of May to inspect the cottage and the lighthouse. I need help putting the house in order now that I've decided to stay. When the inspectors come, they will expect the house to be in order. The lighthouse is fine, but the house, well, you've seen it."

She hesitated. "I don't know the first thing about keeping a house."

He shrugged as if he didn't care either way. "Ida can show you what you don't know."

"We've kissed. We are getting complicated."

He lifted a brow. "Do you want the job or not?"

"I do."

Chapter Fourteen

The next morning, Rachel took stock of the rooms and discovered they were worse than she imagined. Before she'd not noticed the cobwebs, floors in need of waxing or dulled brass. Now she did.

And she didn't have the first idea how to go about it.

Rachel found Ida standing behind the counter balancing her ledgers. The aroma of strong coffee filled the store.

"Ida."

The older woman peered over her glasses. Her eyes were bloodshot and the lines in her face looked deeper. "Lovely wedding don't you think?

"Yes." Rachel's skirts rustled softly as she moved down the isle.

Ida yawned. "I'm getting too old to stay up so

late. The last guests didn't go home until after midnight." She picked up a tin cup beside her and moved to the potbelly stove where a pot of coffee brewed. She poured a cup. "Have one?"

"No thank you."

"Callie and Timothy are staying on the mainland for two days in an Inn."

"I'm so happy for them. They've got their whole lives ahead of them."

"I wouldn't go back to that age for all the gold in the world. I was young and green and when I married my first husband I didn't have the faintest idea of how to be a wife."

Rachel understood only too well. "Every bride has her rose-colored glasses."

Ida stared at Rachel over the rim of her cup. "You are a widow. You should know."

Rachel hesitated. "My marriage was not a success. I wanted it to be, but it failed."

Ida studied her a beat longer. "I'm going to have a talk again today with Mrs. Freely about the school. Yesterday, we caught her by surprise. Now that the idea had had time to sink in she might think differently."

"You don't have to. You see, that's what I've come about. I've gotten a job."

Ida raised a brow. "Doing what?"

"Ben has hired me as his housekeeper."

Ida's gaze swept over Rachel, taking in her porcelain skin and smooth hands. She started to giggle.

"I'm quite serious."

"Yes, I know you are." Tear welled in Ida's eyes as she laughed.

Her ire piqued, Rachel stood taller. "It's not a joke."

"I know." She wiped the tear from her eye. "I suspect you're here for help."

"Yes. How did you know?"

"Oh, I don't know. Most ladies your age who've the time to practice their lace making don't have much in the way of chores to do."

Rachel rubbed her smooth palms. "I don't know the first thing about keeping a home. I've supervised maids and cooks, but I've never done the work. And I must learn these things for myself."

Ida set her cup down on the counter. "All right then, if you're serious."

"I am. I want to make my own way in the world."

"You sound like a lady determined not to go back to her old life."

"I'd die first." Rachel spoke too candidly.

Ida sipped her coffee. "Strong talk."

Rachel straightened her shoulders. "I've made

mistakes. And I'm tired of suffering for them. I want a fresh start."

Ida pulled off her glasses and set them on the counter. "I can appreciate that."

"Then you'll help me?"

"I'll give you your first lesson this morning."

Rachel clapped her hands together. "Excellent."

"Don't get too excited, girl. Your first taste of housework is going to be laundry."

"A simple enough task," Rachel said.

Ida chuckled. "I think you still might have those rose-colored glasses on, girl."

Eight hours later every muscle in Rachel's body ached as she stood behind the cottage watching the sheets, blankets and clothes flap in the cool breeze. Her hands were chapped red by the lye soap and the wind.

That night dinner was a mixed fair of sliced Virginia ham, sliced cheese, day-old bread and coffee. She barely had the energy to eat as she and Ben sat at the small table in the kitchen. Lanterns on the table glowed, casting a soft light on the room.

"You've been busy today." His deep, rusty voice held no hint of fatigue. She'd seen him several times today. He'd hauled a rowboat out of the shed and whitewashed it. He'd chopped wood for the stove. He'd climbed up the lighthouse tower a half-dozen times, hauling oil for the lanterns that fueled the lighthouse beacon. Yet, he didn't look the least bit tired. He looked amused.

"How does one man create so much laundry?"

He tore a piece of ham with his long fingers. "I've not had the chance to send it out in several weeks and the sheets in the spare rooms haven't been done since the last lightkeeper lived here. Let's see…that would be six months."

The muscles in her back groaned. "They smelled of mold and dust."

"I told you you'd had your work cut out for you."

Her eyes felt heavy. The bedroom seemed so far away. "Nothing that can't be handled." With great effort she rose. "I've got sheets to put on the bed and then I'll retire. Ida is retuning in the morning to teach me something about polishing brass."

Ben grimaced. "Good."

Rachel retrieved the sheets from the line outside. The hot sun had dried them and thought they were cold they smelled fresh and clean. She couldn't wait to lie down.

When she returned to the kitchen, Ben had cleaned the plates and put the ham in the pantry.

"You ever made a bed before?" he said.

"How hard can it be to fold sheets over a mattress."

Ben lifted a brow. "I can help."

"No. No. I've got it. This is my job."

She took the bundle and headed to the spare room, which was hers now. She'd moved her belongings in last night when she'd agreed to take the job.

She started with the single bed in her room, reasoning it should be easier to make. Once she'd practiced on her bed, she'd do Ben's.

Of course, the task didn't prove easy. The sheets took on a life of their own. Several times she had to snap the linens to get them to lie flat on the bed. Once she nearly knocked the lantern off the side table. And tucking the corners required more skill than she'd imagined. It took more than a half hour for her to do the one bed. Her back ached and she wanted nothing more than to climb into it.

How hard can it be? She vowed to strike those words from her vocabulary.

"The job will take half as long with two." Ben's voice came from behind her, making her start.

She turned. He stood in the doorway, holding a lantern. His shoulders all but ate up the width of the doorjamb. Suddenly her fatigue faded and her heart beat faster.

Rachel picked up the second bundle. "This is my job. I can do it alone."

Making beds suddenly took on a more intimate

meaning. Vague memories of the night they'd shared after the shipwreck swirled in her head.

He moved toward her. He glanced at the flat steamer trunk where her few possessions sat. He frowned, but said nothing. Rachel had stayed in his room since she'd arrived and Ben had slept in the spare room when he wasn't on duty. However, now that she worked for him, it made sense she take the smaller room.

"Rachel, I'm tired. I'm looking forward to lying on these clean sheets."

She noted then the dark circles under his eyes. He always seemed so strong and capable. It never occurred to her that he would be tired. "Of course."

Together they headed down the hall. The room felt strange now. No longer hers, she felt as though she'd entered dangerous territory.

Ben set the lantern on the nightstand. The light slashed across his face, making him look more like a pirate. The top two buttons of his shirt were unbuttoned, revealing curls of dark hair.

A sharp snap of desire shot through Rachel's limbs. She hugged the sheets closer to her. Don't do this to yourself, she warned.

"Sheets?"

Her head snapped up at the sound of Ben's

voice. He looked amused. And she realized her mouth gaped open. She'd been staring.

Color flooded her cheeks as she dumped the bedclothes on the mattress. Quickly she started to rummage through, looking for the bottom sheet.

Ben reached into the pile. His long fingers brushed hers. Need stabbed inside her. She curled her fingers back, retreating. She'd sailed into dangerous waters.

She cleared the bed of the other linens and set them on top of a chest. When she returned to the bed, Ben had smoothed the sheet on his side flat. She set to work on her side, careful to keep distance between them.

Still, her gaze drifted. Ben's side was military-neat; her side, wrinkled and crooked.

His dark eyes had turned smoky. Tension radiated from his body.

A dozen different emotions tugged at her. With Ben she could find the dark, secret pleasure she'd once heard her maids giggling about—the pleasure she'd never found in Peter's bed. "You've never made a bed before, have you?" His voice was deep, silky.

"No."

"It's been a while for me, too."

Rachel didn't miss the double meaning of his words. A shiver rippled down her spine. She blushed.

She had to get out of this room.

She moved quickly to the trunk and grabbed the top sheet. With a quick snap, the sheet fluttered down over the other.

"You seemed to have found your second wind," Ben said as he tucked the blankets and sheet under the edge of the bed.

She picked up the down pillow. His scent still clung to it. There seemed no escaping him. "Just ready to sleep. I've a busy day tomorrow."

"Can I help you with any other chores?"

She all but jumped out of her skin. "No!"

He chuckled. "Then you best get to bed and get some sleep."

Sleep. Her muscles hummed now and she feared there'd be no sleep tonight.

"Sweet dreams."

Rachel ran from the room and didn't stop until she was in her room and the door shut. She leaned against the closed door.

Ben understood the strength of the connection between them. And he knew, as she did now, that there'd be no avoiding what was going to happen between them.

Peter sat in his study, staring at the reports from the detectives. It had been five weeks since Rachel had disappeared and still there'd been no sign of her. He'd lain awake at night, wondering whom she'd run away with. He knew she couldn't have left alone. She didn't have the spine.

No doubt Rachel and her lover were laughing at him now. He crushed the latest report in his hand and tossed it into the fire.

A light knock sounded on his door. The maid peered inside. "I don't mean to disturb, sir."

"What is it?"

"There is a man to see you, sir."

He curled his fingers into fists. "I don't want to see anyone."

"He says he has news of Mrs. Emmons."

Peter shot to his feet. Few knew that Rachel had left. He'd been careful to keep the information quiet, hoping to salvage his good name. "Where is he?"

The maid flinched. "In the front foyer waiting, sir. His name is Captain LaFortune."

"Send him in."

Peter moved to a side table filled with decanters. He poured himself a bourbon. He took a liberal portion, savoring the way the liquid fire burned his throat. He'd been drinking too much lately.

Seconds later he heard the thud of boots in the hall. He took a sip, forcing himself not to gulp the drink as he stared out the window of his study with his back to the door.

The maid cleared her throat. "Mr. Emmons, may I present Captain LaFortune."

Turning, Peter noted that the man standing in front of him embodied the term "river rat." Dressed in black pants, white lace shirt and a blue jacket with trim, he possessed an arrogance that grated. LaFortune. French, no doubt.

Peter hid his distaste. "You've news of my wife?"

"*Oui,* I do."

Peter lifted an eyebrow. "What makes you think she's missing?"

The captain shrugged. "Perhaps she is not. Perhaps the woman that boarded my ship last month dressed as a widow was not your wife." He reached into his pocket and pulled out Rachel's wedding band.

Peter took the ring. Elation hummed in his veins. For the first time in five weeks he wanted to smile. He held the ruby ring up to the light. The blood-red stones caught the gaslight and blazed. The ring had cost him a fortune. But the cost hadn't mattered. When he'd first seen it, he'd known it would be perfect for Rachel. Damn her. He'd given her the best at every turn and look how she had repaid him.

Peter clenched his hands over the ring until the

stones cut into his palm. "You said a woman boarded your ship?"

"*Oui*. Quite a lovely woman, if I may say. She traded the ring for passage to the Caribbean."

"Was she alone?"

"Yes."

"Where is she?"

The captain shrugged. "That information I must keep to myself until we settle on a price. You see, my ship went down just over a month ago, and I've a mind to replace her."

Peter had the urge to throttle the man. But he'd long ago learned that flies were best caught with honey not vinegar. "How do I know you're telling the truth?"

LaFortune shrugged. "Trust is a wonderful thing, no?"

Peter smiled and poured a second drink. "Yes, it is."

The captain accepted the bourbon, drinking it down in one swallow. "You are a gentleman, that I can see. Let us settle on a price and I will tell you what I know."

Peter went to his desk and drafted a banknote. He handed it to the captain.

The man's eyes widened in surprise before a slow, satisfied smile crossed his lips. He tucked the note into his vest pocket. "She boarded my vessel, the *Anna St. Claire,* just over a month ago. We set sail, but soon we hit rough waters and my ship went down in the Graveyard. For days after the wreck I thought about her, trying to place her in my mind. I read and reread the initials on the inside of the ring. R.E. And then I remembered her. I had seen you two on the New York docks last year."

"What of my wife? Did she go down with the ship?" Had he been cheated of his final reckoning?

"I made inquires among the local fisherman. They'd heard tales of seven men washing up on the shore of the outer banks just south of Corolla. But there was no mention of a woman."

Peter stiffened. "She could have gone down with the ship."

"I thought of that. So I asked more questions. No one spoke of your wife. But one man talked of the lightkeeper's new housekeeper. Quite beautiful. Blond hair, blue eyes."

Peter clenched his fingers. "That could be anyone."

"Ah, but they say she is cultured and has a deep, throaty voice."

Peter's gaze sharpened.

LaFortune smiled. "I think maybe your wife survived."

"Where is this village?"

LaFortune gave him the details. Satisfied, Peter dismissed him and rang for his man of business. When the man entered the room, Peter had opened his safe and counted out cash for his trip.

"Yes, sir?"

"There is a man. LaFortune. He just left here. Find him and detain him. When you receive word from me, kill him."

The man nodded. "Are you preparing for a trip?"

"Why, yes. I'm going to fetch my wife."

Chapter Fifteen

For Ben, keeping his hands off of Rachel the past six weeks was bloody hard. He did his best to maintain his distance, but with each day his awareness of her grew.

At night when he lay in bed, he could hear her moving around her room. He'd imagine her dress sliding from her hips and her slipping naked between the cold sheets. He dreamed of sliding into the same sheets and warming her body.

When she pulled out the tub to wash, he always left the house to give her privacy but that didn't stop him from dreaming of her sitting naked in the tub, the water glistening on her breasts.

Ben shoved out a sigh as he stood on the crow's nest of the lighthouse. Thick gray clouds blanketed the sky. The warm respite with which March had gifted the outer banks had vanished and in its place swept the cold winds of April.

Timothy and Callie had settled into the assistant's quarters. Callie and Rachel had become good friends, each happy to help the other with chores.

Ben looked over the Sound. He saw Sloan's skiff on the dock. The parents were loading up the children for the return trip to the mainland.

He shook his head. The villagers had met again three weeks ago to discuss hiring Rachel. They'd rejected the idea again. To them she was an outsider. Many voiced concerns that she wouldn't stay.

And in truth, he couldn't blame them. He'd been living with Rachel for six weeks now and he didn't know much more about her than he had the day he'd pulled her off the boat.

He'd learned the everyday things about her. He knew she hated waking early; that she liked to collect shells and had lined the windowsill in her room with them; that she hummed when she did the dishes and her nose wrinkled when she laughed. She didn't like the water. But beyond that, he knew nothing more about her past.

He'd done his best to convince himself that the past didn't matter and that it had no hold on them. And most days he believed it, especially when he saw how her mood had lightened over the past few weeks. She hurried from task to task with exuberance, as if making up for lost time.

Only slight traces of the frightened woman remained. However, yesterday Rachel had dropped a plate. The unexpected noise had startled Rachel. When she'd seen the shattered pieces on the floor, he'd seen the fright in her eyes. He'd done his best to calm her worries, but the incident had rattled her.

A splash of blue skirts caught the corner of his eye. He turned to see Rachel heading down the pathway toward the village.

She'd made the trek often in the past few weeks to ask Ida for assistance. Rachel didn't know a damn thing about keeping a home. Without her saying it, he knew that she'd been used to ordering servants around in her former life. She'd come from a privileged and sheltered world. But she hadn't complained. She'd worked hard and when she didn't have an answer she went to Callie or Ida.

Rachel had more salt than he'd first given her credit for.

Through his spyglass he watched the sway of her skirts and the swish of her hair on her shoulders. It was Sunday morning. Everyone would be headed to church now. Where was she going?

He closed the spyglass. He ducked inside the

lighthouse and started down the one hundred and fifty-six spiral steps. He wasn't going into town because Rachel was. After all, he'd promised himself to keep his distance. But he did need to check his mail. He'd written the rescue service and accepted their offer. Their reply should come any day. And, well, if they should bump into each other, then so be it.

He'd take the shortcut around the church and beat her to town.

Ben was whistling as he moved down the steps.

Rachel had stayed away from the church for nearly a year. She'd missed the quiet contemplation and the rousing hymns. This morning when she'd woken up, the day had been so bright and clear. And she'd thought of the little church at the edge of town.

As she moved down the path, the church bell rang, its pure sound echoing over the trees. Her heart felt lighter. It struck her that she'd grown accustomed to making her own decisions. She'd stopped looking over her shoulder and, save for the occasional nightmare, she went days without thinking about her old life.

She thought back to the work she'd done this past month. She'd cleaned and organized the parlor, unpacking all of Ben's boxes. She'd stacked books on the shelves, hung mementos on the wall and put his papers into neat files. The cottage had shaped up nicely.

Puffs of dirt swirled around her ankles as she moved past the collection of small shops toward the church. She wore the dress Ida had given her. She'd laundered the simple cotton two days ago with all the other clothes she'd cleaned. Yesterday, when she'd decided to attend church, she'd borrowed an iron from Callie and spent nearly two hours pressing the wrinkles out of the fine material. She'd scorched a small section of the hem in the back, but otherwise had smoothed the wrinkles out. She'd been pleased with the results.

Most of the villagers had moved into the sanctuary. Horace and Steve stood outside the church, dressed in their everyday work clothes. Their faces, washed clean for church, were tanned and wrinkled by the sun. She'd not seen them since the wedding. Other than Callie and Ida, she'd made no friends. Outsiders simply weren't welcome.

A cold gust of wind blew the flaps of Rachel's skirt. Her stomach twisted in a knot as their gazes locked on her. She smiled. They didn't.

"Good morning," she said, trying again.

Horace grunted. "What are you doing here?"

She paused, just feet from the church steps. Neither man moved.

Rachel lifted her chin. "Excuse me, gentlemen, I don't wish to be late for church." She started to move past them.

Steve blocked her path. Since the night of Callie's reception and her refusal to dance, he'd been cold. "You think you really belong in there?"

She lifted a brow. "Why shouldn't I?"

He spit on the ground. "You're living over at the lighthouse with Ben. We all know that what's going on there ain't right."

"For your information, I am cleaning his house, washing windows and polishing brass."

"Wonder what else she's polishing?" Horace said. The two laughed.

Rachel didn't understand the joke but knew it wasn't flattering. She lifted her skirts and headed up the stairs.

Steve folded his arms. "You ain't going inside. Its just for decent folks."

Their jab irritated her. She'd done nothing wrong. "So is that why you remain outside?"

Her barb hit its mark. Twin sets of eyes narrowed. "Get out of our town," Steve hissed. "We all know it's just a matter of time before you leave."

"I work for Ben now."

Horace stepped toward her. "That damn Yank had his eyes set for my Molly before you arrived. Everyone expected them to marry. She's one of us, like him."

Rachel remembered the buxom redhead from the party. "I've done nothing to interfere with whatever match between your Molly and Ben."

He hooked his thumb into his waistband. "Well, you have. She ain't had the nerve to deliver one cake or pie to his cottage since you arrived."

Rachel shrugged. "That's her choice, not mine."

Horace kicked the sandy dirt with his feet. "You're interfering where you're not welcome." He leaned forward a fraction. "Maybe you're just the kind of woman who enjoys twisting a man around her finger."

His cruel words struck a nerve. They smacked of something Peter would have said. A black cloud passed in front of the sun. The chill in the air bit through her shawl.

"What kind of game are you playing?" Steve demanded.

"Game?" This was absurd. "I'm trying to live my life." They'd never let her in the church.

"Then do it somewhere else. You ain't welcome here."

"Apologize, Horace." Ben's deep voice was sharp with anger as he strode around the side of the church.

The wind tossed Ben's hair and flapped the edges of his open coat. His broad shoulders showed confidence and ease, a man comfortable in his environment. But, she imagined, he would be confident anywhere.

He'd kept his distance from her these past few weeks and she realized she'd missed him.

The two men, startled by Ben's arrival, took a step back. "We're just speaking the truth," Horace said.

"Didn't sound that way to me," Ben retorted. His face looked fierce. "Sounded like bullying."

"She needs to hear the truth," Horace said, his face red with anger. "No one wants her here."

"No one? Or just you and your wife?" Ben's voice was low and dangerous.

"You and Molly planned to marry!" Horace balled his fingers into fists.

"Marriage was never discussed. We are simply friends."

"That's not how she tells it."

Ben shrugged. He didn't call Molly a liar but his body language did.

Horace bared his teeth. He lunged at Ben, taking a swing.

Ben moved quickly, dodging Horace's strike. Horace stumbled to the ground. However, Ben didn't see Steve's swing. The sucker punch caught Ben on the side of his face.

Eyes blazing with fury, Ben whirled around and drove his fist into Steve's gut. The man doubled over. Ben hauled him to his feet. He struck him on the jaw.

Steve crumpled to the ground, rolling on his side, his lip bleeding.

Rachel stepped back. The violence stunned her. She saw flashes of Peter.

Horace sat up, sneering at Rachel's pale features. "Your lady friend looks afraid of you, Ben."

Ben's gaze pinned Rachel. Anger still blazed in his eyes.

A cold, savage fear tightened her insides. She'd never seen this side of him before.

Ben reached out to her.

Rachel looked at the blood on his knuckles and ran.

Ben found Rachel on the pier. Her arms crossed over her chest, she stood at the end, staring out over the darkening sky. Rage still fresh from his fight pumped through his veins.

"Rachel." Tension radiated from each syllable.

She turned immediately. She glanced around, wanting to leave, but quickly realized she was trapped. He hated the haunted look in her eyes; hated it more that he'd put it there.

"We need to talk," he said.

She stiffened. "What is there to say? You hit that man, *twice.*"

"Damn right I did. He threw a cheap shot. I lost my temper."

"You're not sorry."

"No." And he added without softening, "I'd do it again."

She whitened.

"I won't apologize for defending myself."

"You didn't have to hit him."

"What was I supposed to do, Rachel? Tell him to play nice?"

She wrapped her arms around her chest. "I don't know. I just didn't expect you to be so violent." She moistened her lips.

His gaze burned her. "I make no apologies for defending myself."

A tear slid down her cheek.

Ben could read her thoughts. "I'm not *him.*"

Shock glistened in her eyes. "What?"

"You're comparing me to that bastard husband of yours. I'm not him."

"Aren't you?" she blurted, a bit hysterical.

"I won't allow men like Steve, Horace or a foolish diplomat to run over me or my men because I'm too afraid to fight. I don't go looking for fights, but if one finds me, I damn well meet it head-on."

She cringed and he realized he'd shouted the last words.

Suddenly the anger in him evaporated. How had this day turned so sour? All he'd wanted to do was to enjoy this day with her.

"You and I fit, Rachel. You've felt it from the start and so have I."

"You kissed me and I liked it. That's hardly a foundation for a lifetime together. The truth is that we really don't know each other."

"Who's fault is that?" The anger had burned itself out. Now there was only the need to touch her.

She tensed, a clear sign she wasn't ready for his touch. "I'll make no apologies for protecting myself."

He lifted a brow. "Yet you expect me to apologize for doing the same."

Her fingers curled into fists. "That was different."

"Was it? I'll wager you'd have landed a punch to protect yourself now."

She glanced down at her clenched fingers.

"When you first arrived, you were frightened

and scared. You're not anymore. Now you are a fighter."

The truth of his words struck home. "I don't know what I'd do."

Lord, but he wanted to hold her. "I dream about you at night," he admitted.

Her eyes widened.

"Aye, every night since you arrived. I dream of taking you to my bed and touching you. I care deeply about you, Rachel. I'd never hurt you."

She tilted her head back. Still, more tears streamed down her face. "That's what *he* said."

"I'm not him."

"Evil has many faces."

Her words stunned him. "Do you really think that I am evil?"

Her watered gaze held his for a long moment. "No."

"Do you think that I'd ever hurt you?"

She hesitated. "I don't know." Her softening gaze belied her words.

"Rachel. Think back to that first night you were here. I held you in my arms to warm your body. We lay naked together all night. I could have done anything to you that night and you'd have been unable to stop me. What would *he* have done?"

The pain in her eyes gave him his answer. If he

could dig the monster up and kill him all over again, he would.

Ben took a small step toward her. This time she did not retreat. "I am not him," he repeated softly.

Rachel pushed beyond her fear and listened to Ben's words. The fight in town had frightened her. The sound of flesh hitting flesh had churned too many memories that she'd thought she'd been able to put aside.

She looked down at his hands. Dried blood caked the knuckles of his right hand. In the distance, Rachel heard the church bells. The service had ended. Soon people would be headed to the docks.

Ben stood in front of her, tall, proud, noble. He wore a black cable-knit sweater, dark coat and pants. Some might have thought him formidable, standing on the pier, his feet braced apart. But she saw beyond the hardness.

There was kindness in his eyes when he looked at her. When he touched her, he was gentle not cruel.

He wasn't afraid to defend right and wrong.

He wasn't a perfect man. Which perhaps was good. She had her own secrets. Her own flaws. "I don't want to be afraid anymore," she said.

He opened his arms, a quiet invitation.

She couldn't marry him, but she could love him. *Love.* The word was foreign to her. She'd never loved a man romantically. But she knew now that she loved Ben Mitchell.

With two steps, she closed the distance between them. He wrapped his arms around her and held her close to him. His heat enveloped her. He smelled of sea and fresh air.

He pulled back, tipped her chin up with his fingers. His eyes darkened. Then slowly he lowered his lips to hers.

The kiss was gentle at first. A testing of the waters. But like a flint against stone, it sparked and started a fire within her.

She raised up on tiptoes and wrapped her arms around his neck. He tasted so good. She opened her mouth and without hesitation he pushed his tongue into her.

"I want you," he said, his lips against her mouth as if he couldn't stop touching her. "Come back to the cottage with me."

Chapter Sixteen

Ben's heart jumped when Rachel blushed and looked up at him. "I'd like that."

He kissed her again, cursing the mile-long walk back to his cottage. A dark, primitive side of him demanded he toss her over his shoulder and take her up to the inn. He'd lock the door and make love to her until both were satiated. Two or three days, minimum.

Instead he took her by the hand. Rachel deserved a gentle, slow lovemaking. Later, when she'd banished her fears, he'd show her lovemaking could be just as good when hot and passionate.

He smiled.

She leaned close to him. "What are you smiling about?"

"Just thinking about all the different kinds of

ways I can make love to you. And that I've got a lifetime to show them all."

Her throaty laughed stroked his senses. "I would very much like to know them all."

He wrapped his arm around her shoulders and pulled her close. "You are sure about this?"

"I've made mistakes. But this won't be one of them."

Her gentle reply hit him square in the gut. God, but he wanted her.

Together they walked off the pier. They strolled along the sandy path and passed another dock. The wind howled around her skirts. She glanced up at the sound. The clouds had thickened.

In the distance she saw Sloan's boat. It bobbed in the water like a cork. The children sat huddled together to fight off the wind. "Today doesn't look like a good day for a crossing."

Ben's gaze trailed hers. He muttered an oath. The desire that had singed his veins vanished in a wave of concern. "It's not."

"Why would they send the children back to the mainland today?"

"The fools don't want the children to miss a day of school."

Rachel hugged her arms. "Everyone is in

church. Perhaps we should tell them the children should return."

A wave crashed over the bow of Sloan's boat. In the distance she heard the children squeal with fear. "It'll be too late." Ben glanced toward the end of the dock. A dory moored beside it bobbed up and down. "I'm going after them."

Rachel stared at the sea. Whitecaps dotted the water. Her stomach tightened. Lord, but she hated being out on the water. "I'm going with you."

Ben shook his head. "Go to the church. Warn the families about the change in the water. There are twelve children out there. I'll need help."

Rachel wanted to be by Ben's side. She wanted to help. But saving the children took precedence over her wishes. "Please be careful."

He touched her face with his hand. "Don't worry."

Tears pooled in her eyes as she picked up her skirts and ran down the path. Don't cry! She sniffed, annoyed that she couldn't stay as calm and controlled as Ben. The wind speed picked up. The sky seemed to grow darker by the moment.

Church had finished, but everyone would be milling out the double doors, never thinking to cast an eye toward the Sound.

Rachel kept running. Her side began to hurt. As

the path reached the main road, she looked up ahead and saw two men and a women.

She shouted, "Please, we need your help."

The three turned. Steve, Horace Freely, his wife Marianne. Steve's blackened right eye had closed shut. Marianne dabbed a handkerchief to his bruised lip. Both the men took a step back as if they expected Ben to be nearby.

"We don't want no trouble," Mrs. Freely said. "Ben made his point. We'll speak to you with respect. And my brother won't be throwing any more punches." She spoke loudly, glancing around as if she expected Ben to materialize.

Horace groaned. "Sorry for what we said," he said.

Rachel stopped in front of them. She dug her fingertips into her aching side. "The Sound," she said breathless. "The children are on the Sound."

Steve nodded. "Yeah, yeah. We sent them back to school this morning."

Mrs. Freely stopped dabbing her brother's lip. Her gaze burned into her. "What about the children?"

The cold air burned Rachel's lungs. "The wind has shifted. The water is rough. Sloan's boat looks to be taking on water."

Mrs. Freely paled. The wrinkles around her eyes deepened. "Oh, dear Lord."

Horace's eyes widened. "Are the children all right?"

"The boat hasn't capsized, but Ben fears it might. He's already headed out into the Sound."

Steve snatched the handkerchief and shoved it into his pocket. His eyes hardened with worry. "Horace, we can take my fishing boat. It's bigger than yours. Marianne, go back to town and tell the folks what's happening."

Mrs. Freely's eyes filled with tears. "Molly didn't want to go this morning. She and I had another fight about school. She wouldn't kiss me goodbye before she got on the boat."

Horace squeezed her hand. "Don't fret, Marianne, she's tough and smart. I'll bring her home safe."

Steve nodded. "Let's go."

Mrs. Freely ran toward town and the men started down the path toward another dock. Rachel followed the men. She could be more help out on the water.

Rachel looked out toward the Sound. Sloan's boat had lost its sail. The water had started to pitch and roll. Ben's dory was halfway to the children's boat.

Horace and Steve ran to the end of the sun-baked dock. Rachel started to follow. She quickly discovered planks were spilt in many places. She could feel the motion of the water and see the waves rolling under a rotted pier slat. The motion of the water made her dizzy.

Horace shouted an order to Steve. Rachel looked up. They were untying the line.

Sucking in a deep breath, she ran the length of the dock, praying she didn't fall into the water. "I'm coming with you."

Horace groaned. "Stay put, lady. We don't need any more trouble."

With a trembling hand, Rachel reached for the ladder that led down to the boat. "I'm coming." She climbed down.

Please don't let me fall. Please don't let me fall.

She chanted the words as her foot touched the wobbly bottom of the boat. She released the rung. And lost her balance.

Steve grabbed her by the arm and unceremoniously dropped her onto a plank seat. "You looking to drown, lady?"

Rachel clenched her fists. "I sincerely hope not."

Horace's face was ashen with worry as he pushed away from the dock. He started to row.

In the distance the church bell began to ring faster, its tone a frantic shout for help.

Rachel's knuckles whitened with each stroke of the oar as they moved further from shore.

Thoughts of the sinking *Anna St. Claire* coiled around her. Horace rowed as fast as he could but she feared it would not be fast enough. The waves licked over the side of the children's boat. It rocked and pitched.

Less than a hundred feet separated Ben from the children. Horace and Steve, working together, moved at a faster clip than Ben's boat. They were closing in on him and Sloan's boat quickly.

Water sloshed around Rachel's feet. Sea spray hit her in the face. Her stomach churned.

The children's shouts drifted over the water. And from the shore, the people shouted back. The whole village stood on the sandy banks now. She could all but imagine how helpless the parents felt watching their children in such dangerous waters.

Rachel gripped the sides of the boat, twisting in her seat so that she could get a better view ahead. A gust of wind whipped across the water. Sloan's boat pitched violently. Then it capsized.

Ben dug his oars into the water as if Hades himself had come to claim his soul.

Just feet from the boat, he heard the gust of wind. He rode out the waves that followed, but heard the children's screams and splash of Sloan's boat.

Ben immediately saw nine children slapping

against the surface of the water. He started to haul them into his dory. First Mary Kelly, thirteen years old—she was soaked and crying. Then came Tucker and Billy, both five years old. Next, Jackson, Matthew, McKenzie, Joshua, Max and Sandy.

The children were packed into the dory, which now rode low on the water's edge. They all huddled together, crying.

Ben looked at Mary Kelly, the oldest. "How many children were on the boat?"

Her teeth chattered. "Twelve."

"Are you sure?"

She closed her eyes and continued to cry. "Yes, I think so."

He tamped down the fire burning in him. "You've got to be, honey."

She sniffed. "Yes, there were twelve."

Horace's boat reached them then. His larger vessel skimmed alongside the dory. "How many?"

"We're missing three," Ben shouted. He saw Rachel in the back of the boat. Her pale skin looked ghostly but she sat tall. She hated the water, yet she'd come. He tore his gaze from her. "Horace, get the children into your boat. I'm going in to look for the others."

"Where's my son, Johnny?" Horace choked.

"I don't know," Ben admitted.

Pain etched the deep lines in the fisherman's face. "I can't swim."

Ben dove into the Sound. The icy waters burned his skin. Salt water stung his eyes and mouth as he swam toward the underside of the boat. With luck the children were trapped in the air pocket underneath.

He swam, cutting through the dark waters until he saw two sets of kicking legs. Ben swam up toward the capsized boat. His lungs ached. He needed air.

He swam up and broke through the air pocket. The two children held on to the edge of the boat, their faces barely above the water. At the rate they were crying and screaming, the air would not last.

"Emma and Ruth, I need for you to hold your breath. We're swimming to the surface."

"Johnny is missing," Emma said, spitting out water as she struggled to keep her head up.

Ben tossed a look over his shoulder. The child wasn't here. He swallowed a hard lump. "Where's Sloan?"

"The boom hit him on the head. He went overboard."

Ben digested the information. "Let's get up." He looked at the girl's frightened eyes. "Hold hands and don't let go. I'll pull you all to the surface. On the count of three. One, two, three."

They sucked in a breath and together the four of them ducked under the water.

Rachel scanned the waters for signs of the children and Ben. The waves pitched and swayed. The clouds grew darker.

"I'm cold." A little girl looked up at her, her eyes bright with fear.

Rachel pulled off her coat and wrapped it around the girl and the child next to her. She rubbed their arms. "You'll be home soon."

"I want my mama," the youngest child said.

Rachel smiled. "You'll see her soon enough."

"Look out there!" another child shouted.

Rachel looked. Fifteen feet from the boat, a child floated to the surface. It was Johnny. She rose.

"Johnny!" She glanced wildly around the boat.

Horace's head snapped up. "I've got to get to him. I can't swim."

Steve followed Horace's gaze. "We've got to wait for Ben and the other children."

Tears filled Horace's eyes. "My son!"

Rachel didn't stop to think. She lifted her skirts and jumped into Ben's dory.

Pushing through the water, Ben hauled the girls toward the surface. They each clamped their eyes closed but they kicked hard. They were fighters.

Ben and the girls surfaced in time to see Rachel rowing the boat. Her strokes were choppy and uneven, but the dory was making slow progress.

Handing the girls to Horace, Ben swam toward Rachel. He reached her just as she had reached the child. She set down her oars and leaned over the edge of the dory. The boy was just out of reach. She leaned further, straining her body and stretching her fingertips. Water splashed on her chest and into her mouth. The dory was going to tip over.

She grabbed Johnny's brown coat and hauled him up. Unconscious and drenched, he weighed too much for her. "Help!"

Ben reached the boat and grabbed Johnny's lifeless body by his coat collar. He handed him up to Rachel and then swung his own body into the boat.

Immediately Rachel lay the boy on the bottom and turned him onto his side. She pushed his long hair off his face as water trickled from his nose and mouth. Setting him on his back, she tipped his head back and started to blow in his mouth.

Ben watched, surprised she knew what to do. Then he thought about her love of books. She'd read this somewhere.

Johnny's lips were blue. And Ben feared there'd be no saving the boy. She blew air into his mouth. His lungs rose and fell.

Ben pushed her aside. "Let me." He turned the boy onto his side again and hit him between the shoulder blades hard.

Johnny lay still.

Rachel started to weep.

Ben struck him again.

This time, the boy's nostrils moved. A shallow cough escaped his lips. And then he inhaled a deep, sharp breath.

Johnny stared breathing deep, even breaths. He opened his eyes and looked up at Ben. "Am I in trouble?"

Ben laughed as he wiped the water from the boy's face. "No, son, you're not."

Rachel scooped up the boy and wrapped her arms around him to give him her warmth. "You gave us quite a scare."

"Ahoy," Horace shouted.

"The boy's fine," Ben shouted. "Sloan?"

Horace shook his head.

Ben stared at Rachel. She had red, watery eyes, her hair plastered against her face. And she'd never looked more beautiful.

He knew he loved her.

* * *

They reached the shore in fifteen minutes, the wind with Ben as he rowed. Horace's vessel was faster and he glided with the children into the dock minutes before him. The sounds of parents and children crying drifted over the water.

All twelve children were accounted for, but Sloan was lost. Several of the older children had seen him go overboard. Likely his body would wash up on shore by dusk.

The mothers and fathers took their children, each dripping wet and terrified. The children would all recover, including Johnny, who'd already picked a fight with his cousin Ruth.

Rachel was happy to put her feet on dry land. She knew if she lived to be one hundred, she'd never become accustomed to the water.

Ben laid his hands on her shoulders. His warm fingers tightened. "You scared me to death," he breathed against her ear.

She leaned back into him. Touching him made her feel safe and alive. "I didn't think."

He turned her around, his face tight with worry. "For my sake, don't take a chance like that again."

Rachel leaned her forehead against his chest. "I will try to be more careful, Mr. Mitchell."

He wrapped his arms around her chest. "You all right?"

"Freezing, but fine."

His heart beat faster. "I don't think I could live without you."

She hugged him tighter. "Nor I you."

He rested his chin on the top of her head. Seconds passed as they held each other.

"I've got just the thing to warm you up," he said. The husky, seductive tone in his voice warmed her blood.

She could never give herself to him in marriage, but he had her heart forever. She would give what she had and pray that it was enough.

Peter hated to travel by rail. The station was crowded with hundreds of mindless people milling around with not a care that they were bumping into him. A baby's cry pierced his brain.

Added to that, the trains were slow, often late and the seats even in this exclusive car uncomfortable. Traveling by sea, he controlled everything. On the train he felt like cattle.

He rose from the plush club chair and walked to the small bar. His gold wedding band winked in the light. He poured himself a whiskey. Glancing out the window, he tapped his ring against the glass tumbler as he stared at the flat, barren land of southern Virginia. Farming country.

In three hours they'd be in North Carolina. There he'd catch a coach and then a boat to the coastal town.

He rolled the crystal tumbler in his hands. He thought back to the last five weeks—the sleepless nights, the tortuous images of Rachel in another man's arms. "Rachel, you've put me to quite a lot of trouble."

But soon he would find her and set things right. She would understand that she'd made a grave error running form him. *Until death us do part, my love.*

He thought about ropes he'd packed in his bag, the blindfold and the small knives. "Our reunion is going to be very special. Very special indeed."

Chapter Seventeen

Rachel was nervous and excited as Ben lit the lantern.

The lantern light glowed softly on her skin as Ben moved toward her. They stood facing each other in his bedroom, curtains drawn, barefoot, each silent and lost in their own thoughts. A fire crackled and hissed in the hearth.

Ben set the second lantern on the table beside the bed and looked down at Rachel. He traced her jawline with his index finger. Shivers danced down her spine. "Turn around. You've got to get out of that wet dress."

She turned. "I've heard that story before."

He chuckled as his fingers brushed the ends of her hair forward over her shoulder, and then fumbled with the top button. He quickly worked his way down the row. "It's a marvel you were able to get this dress on," he said, chuckling.

"Years of practice."

He peeled the fine fabric forward until her bodice hung at her waist. Cupping her bare shoulders, he kissed the back of her neck. Her heart raced.

Rachel pushed her dress to the floor, stepped out of it and faced him. Her chemise clung to her full breasts and flat belly. By rights she should have been freezing, but she was warm. Very warm.

Ben's eyes darkened as his gaze slid to the hard peaks of her nipples. He pulled off his sweater and tossed in onto the floor beside her dress. Water droplets glistened in the thick mat of hair that tapered down over his flat belly and below his belt.

His body looked as if it had been forged from marble. A Greek god. Every sinewy muscle well defined under his taught skin. Her mouth watered at the sight of him. "You are beautiful," she whispered.

The yearning inside her made her bold. She reached for his belt buckle and unclasped it. She unbuttoned his pants.

He grabbed her hand and kissed her fingertips. White teeth glistened in the soft light. "Ah, lass, be careful. We don't want this adventure over before it starts."

She nibbled her lip. "Did I do something wrong?"

"Nay."

"Show me what you like," she whispered.

He tugged the ribbons between her breasts and released the gauzy fabric. Without hesitating, he tugged the fabric free and let the chemise fall. She slid off her pantaloons and stepped out of them. She stood naked in front of him, but felt no shame. In fact, nothing had ever felt more right.

Ben picked her up and carried her to his bed. He laid her on the clean blankets and quickly stripped his pants off.

Seeing him fully naked, aroused, gave her pause. The full weight of what was to come hit her.

Tonight she would commit herself to this man. Once they made love there'd be no going back. She would love him forever and always.

And her love would be stronger than any vow.

The mattress sagged under his weight as he lay beside her, the gleam in his eye sure and knowing. "I don't want you to think about him."

Startled she met his gaze. "What?"

He tipped her chin up so that her gaze met his. "I won't ever hurt you. It will be good between us."

His features had softened. She could see that he cared for her. "I know that it will."

"If you aren't ready, we can wait," he said softly.

And she knew that he would. "I want this. I want this more than anything."

He smoothed her hair off her face. "You are the beauty. A gift from Neptune himself."

She laughed. "Like a mermaid."

He traced his finger over her flat belly. "Nay, a beautiful siren sent to tempt my soul."

"Ah, but if you heard my singing, you might not be so tempted."

He chuckled, but the laughter in his eyes quickly turned serious. "I've not been the same since I first laid eyes on you."

"Nor I you."

He kissed her.

Rachel melted into the kiss. Her soul opened up, savoring the taste of him. The residual emotions from today's rescue had heightened her senses, but this kiss, this wondrous kiss, sent her soaring.

She pulled her fingertips over his broad shoulders and down his back. He moaned, deepening the kiss.

Ben rose up on his elbows. He smoothed her hair back. "Your hair is like silk," he muttered.

He kissed the tip of her nose, her chin and the hollow of her neck. Slowly he trailed kisses down her chest until he reached her breast. He suckled her nipple until it formed a hard peak.

Rachel arched back. She couldn't think. This was deliciously wicked, sensual. She threaded her fingers through is thick hair. Slowly her hands trailed down his back. This time she cupped his buttocks.

He kissed her again, devouring her mouth. His legs brushed hers as he brought his knee up and gently prodded her thighs open. Opening her legs, she widened the breach. His hardness settled on her moist center, his flesh pressing against her.

He cupped her face. The gleam in his eye turned voracious. "Promise me."

It took a moment for her mind to register that he'd spoken. Her body hummed with such excitement. She longed for a release she didn't quite understand. "Anything."

"Marry me," he said.

He deserved the truth from her. Yet as she stared at his dark eyes, he began to move back and forth so that his hardness rubbed against her outer flesh. Common sense fled. She needed this one night with him. "I will love you forever with my whole heart."

Her words caught him off guard. "You *love* me." Pride laced each word.

"More than I thought possible." And she did.

He moved on top of her, his actions impatient as if he wished to claim her for fear she'd vanish.

Rachel craved him. She arched her back, pressing her center to his. He pushed into her slowly. Her very tight folds wrapped around him. He expelled a breath, savoring her heat.

Slowly he began to move. His kisses had sparked a fire in her that exploded into a blaze. Her body throbbed with wanting. She raised her legs and wrapped them around him, accepting all that he had to offer.

When his fingertips moved to her moist center she thought she'd go mad with wanting. He moved inside her as he stroked her. The sensations welled up like a great tidal storm. And then, without warning, her senses exploded. She tipped over an imaginary line, calling his name as she fell into a hot, satisfying pool of sensations.

Ben groaned her name. He tensed and found his release, collapsing against her.

They fell asleep together, wrapped in each other's arms.

Ben woke before Rachel. The sun had set and shadows shrouded the room. The fire crackled in the hearth.

He rolled onto his side and stared at her profile. The light from the fire flickered on her pale skin, her aquiline nose and full, rosy lips.

She'd come alive in his arms when they'd made love. He'd seen the shock and pleasure in her eyes when he'd touched her and then brought her passion into full bloom.

Rachel moistened her lips. Her breathing was deep and even. She enjoyed the kind of rest usually felt by only those with a light heart.

He traced her nose with his fingertip. "I will cherish you forever."

Her eyes fluttered open. She focused on him and her gaze softened. "You are staring at me."

Ben grinned. "I will never tire of looking at you."

She touched her mouth. "I can't imagine what I look like when I sleep. I hope I didn't snore."

He lifted a brow. "Yes, you did," he teased. "In fact, you woke me."

Shock widened her eyes. "You're joking! Aren't you?" Her cheeks reddened. "I never imagined myself a snorer."

God, but she charmed him. He couldn't let the farce continue. "You weren't snoring, my love."

She sat up on her elbows. The sheet fell away from her breasts. He forgot all about teasing. "Are you quite certain?"

His arousal hardened. He traced a circle around her nipple. It grew taught. "I promise, you are a quiet angel when you sleep."

Her soft curls grazed the top of her shoulders. "Thank heavens."

With a groan he pulled her down to the pillow. He straddled her. "I can't get enough of you."

She smiled, sliding her foot along his leg. His body burned.

He kissed her, losing himself in the taste of her. He felt her arms wrap around his neck. Her breasts pressed into his chest.

"I'll never get enough of you, either," she whispered. She opened her legs.

This time when he drove into her, a fever pulsed in his veins. Their coupling was quick, fast and hard. And very, very satisfying.

Just past midnight, Rachel awoke. Ben was dressed and kneeling by the hearth, lacing his boots.

Rachel sat up, holding the sheet over her breasts. "Where are you going?"

He lifted his head. White teeth flashed when he met her gaze. "I've got the midnight-to-dawn shift tonight."

"I don't want you to leave." The bed already felt cold without him.

He rose and crossed to her. "I will be back before you wake again. Then we will have all day tomorrow to enjoy ourselves."

The idea warmed her blood. "If only we could stay in this room forever. The world outside only complicates everything."

He cupped her face. "The world gets in the way sometimes, but what is between us is simple and pure."

She smiled. "Simple and pure."

"I have something for you," he said. He opened the small drawer on the nightstand. He pulled out a tiny, black-velvet sack. He opened the drawstring and pulled out a delicate gold ring engraved with dogwood leaves. The gold glistened in the firelight.

Rachel sat straighter.

Ben took her left hand in his and placed the ring in the palm of her hand. "It belonged to my mother. It was her wedding ring."

Rachel's chest tightened. "Ben."

"Rachel Davis, will you marry me?" He held the ring between his fingers.

She accepted the ring. The polished gold glittered in the firelight.

She had never felt happier. And more sad.

A heavy silence hung between them.

"It's a simple ring," Ben said.

"It's a lovely ring." For an instant she imagined the ring on her finger. She dreamed of a simple wedding in the village chapel, of babies…and of a long life together. "I can't accept it." She held the ring out to him.

He stance stiffened. "Why not?"

Tears pooled in her eyes.

"Is it this village? The life by the sea? Me?"

"It's none of those." Her throat tightened with emotion. "There's something I never told you."

"About *him*." His voice was hoarse with anger.

"Yes."

He knelt in front of her and laid his hands on her knees. "What he did to you is the past, Rachel. It can't touch us."

The tenderness in his voice nearly undid her. "Yes, it can."

He wiped a tear from her cheek. "Tell me."

She met his gaze. "I ran away."

"I know."

"From my husband."

Ben stared at her as if he hadn't heard her right. "Husband?"

"I am still married."

The gentleness vanished from his eyes.

It pained her to know she'd robbed him of the joy he'd felt moments ago. She lifted her chin, refusing to cry anymore. "Peter and I have been married almost a year." She wiped a tear from her face.

"The abuse was subtle at first, but it got worse very quickly. The last day we were together he hit me so hard I lost consciousness. The next morning after he left for a business trip, I packed a bag and ran."

"That's why you were on the freighter."

"Yes."

Ben rose, his shoulders stiff. He jabbed his hands through his hair. "You should have told me."

"At first I was afraid. And then, as I started to have feelings for you, I knew if I told you, you would look at me differently. I didn't want to lose the connection between us."

He shoved the ring into his pocket as if he couldn't bear to look at it.

"Damn it, Rachel," he muttered. "You should have told me."

"I wanted to. But I was so afraid. Peter is a wealthy man. He'd pay dearly for my return."

His jaw tightened, released, tightened again. "You should have trusted *me*."

"I know."

He strode toward the door.

"Where are you going?" she asked.

"To the light."

"Will you be back?"

"At dawn." He opened the door and paused. "Its

best you pack your belongings and move into town. Ida will see that you have a bed."

Without a word, he closed the door.

Peter arrived in the small coastal town minutes past midnight. The trip had been grueling. But he would keep going. He was too close to stop now.

The coachman set the brake and tied off his reins. "Waverly, North Carolina."

Peter looked out the window. The town was pitch-black except for lanterns burning inside the tavern. Good. He'd asked them to wait up for him. So few people knew how to follow directions these days.

The coachman tossed Peter's bag on the dirt road.

Peter cringed at the fool's mistreatment of his luggage. The leather bag cost more than the cretin made in a decade. However, Peter kept his temper in check. He needed information.

He climbed down from the coach. His bones ached.

The town matched LaFortune's descriptions exactly.

He was so close to his Rachel. So close.

Rachel was numb.

She didn't remember dressing or collecting her few belongings. A lantern in her hand, she'd walked along the path toward the village. Ben had told her to leave in the morning, but she couldn't bare to stay in his cottage another moment. Everything reminded her of him—his shirt draped over a chair, his scent on the sheets and his shoes lined up by the bureau.

She reached the town and walked down the sandy street toward Ida's store. She tripped over a root and nearly stumbled.

Suddenly the tears that had been choking her throat for the last hour spilled. She sat on a crate in front of the inn. Great sobs shook her body. She stared up into the stars.

She'd lived for years without love. They'd been lonely, empty years, but never having tasted love, they had been tolerable. Now that her heart had opened, that she'd tasted true happiness, to go on without it…the loneliness stretched ahead of her as endless as the ocean.

A light came on in the store. She heard footsteps. Too exhausted to care, she didn't bother to dry her eyes. The front door opened.

Ida. Her lantern glowed, illuminating her white nightgown. Her silver-gray hair hung in a long braid and she wore a shawl around her shoulders.

Rachel took in a breath. She sat straighter, but didn't speak for fear she'd break down again.

Sighing, Ida moved out into the cold and sat next to her. "You two have been an accident waiting to happen."

Rachel sniffed. "I've made a terrible mess of things."

"What happened?"

"Ben asked me to marry him."

"And you said no?"

She nodded.

Ida's eyes narrowed. "You love him."

Rachel wiped another tear from her face. "With all my heart."

"But…"

"I'm married."

Ida blew out a breath. "I knew it."

"How?"

Ida pinched the bridge of her nose. "I saw myself in you."

Rachel swiped a tear away. "I don't understand."

"My first husband wasn't a good man. He was a drinker and when he had too much, he hit me."

"What did you do?"

"For a time, I took it. Time came when I couldn't tolerate it anymore. So I left him. I reached the point where I didn't care about the scandal and I would have divorced him if I'd had the money. I got a job in town working in this very store. We lived separate lives for almost six years before he died. During that six-year stretch, I met my second husband. He owned the store. We were together for twenty happy years before I lost him."

"Peter will not allow me to live without him." Rachel told Ida about her marriage.

The old woman nodded, the lines in her face growing deeper.

"If I try to divorce Peter, he will find me. If he finds me, he will kill me."

Ida tapped her foot. "Out here the laws of society have a tendency to blur. A man and woman who love each other…well, no one would ask too many questions if they decided to build a home together."

"Ben wants marriage."

"Ben loves you."

"He's so angry."

"Give him time. Most men need to crawl off and sulk for a while. When their temper cools, they often see things differently."

"I will never forget the look in his eyes."

"Don't let that look be the last memory you have of him, Rachel. Go back to the lighthouse and set things right."

"Do you really think we can work this out?"

"I don't know. But don't you think you owe it

to Ben and yourself to try? Let this chance pass and you will regret it for the rest of your life."

Rachel nodded. "You're right."

Ida patted her on the knee. "Come inside and get a good night's sleep. You can head back to the cottage first thing."

Rachel shook her head. "No, I must do this now."

"It's nearly one in the morning."

She glanced toward the lighthouse beacon. It flashed bright and strong. Ben was up there alone. Hurting.

"I'm going now."

Ida's gaze softened with respect. "Well, get a move on, girl."

Rachel hugged the older woman. "Thank you."

She hurried down the street. She was in such a rush she didn't notice the shadow on the other side of the street. Or the fact that it moved behind her.

Rachel reached the end of the boardwalk and started toward the path when she heard the snap of a twig behind her.

An odd sensation stopped her in her tracks. She felt as if evil had passed by her. She turned.

Peter stood on the path. "Hello, Rachel. Miss me?"

Chapter Eighteen

Ben gripped the cold rail of the crow's nest, staring out over the ocean. The icy wind stung his face. The lighthouse beacon flashed behind him.

Damn her! She'd had plenty of chances over the past six weeks to tell him about her husband. *Husband*. Dear God. She could have told him. Instead, she'd let him fall in love with her knowing she could never be his.

And damn him for ignoring the signs that had been in front of his face since the day he'd pulled her from the wreck. Hell, he'd challenged her about her widow's weeds but she'd shouted that her husband had died.

The truth had been there all along and he'd looked the other way.

Restless, Ben turned from the ocean and went

inside the lighthouse. He glanced up the narrow stairway that led to the giant Frensel lenses in the light chamber. They flashed bright.

His watch didn't end for another four hours. He should stay. He'd never ignored his duty, even in the vilest weather. Yet, tonight, he didn't care about duty or honor. He'd played by the rules of honor and lost first to the Navy and now Rachel.

He started down the one hundred and fifty-six steps. His heart pounded in his chest. Conflicting emotions, so strong now, robbed the breath from him. He thought only to get outside and to see Rachel.

Bounding down the stairs, he dashed across the yard to the lightkeeper's cottage. He burst through the back door, expecting to see her in the kitchen brewing a pot of tea or sitting at the table mending one of his shirts.

She wasn't in the kitchen. He hurried through the house calling her name. He pushed open the door to his bedroom. Nothing. The sheets were still rumpled from their lovemaking, but she'd vanished.

Rachel was gone.

He crossed the room and touched the sheets. Just hours ago they'd lain between these sheets making love. Her scent still clung to them.

He remembered how she'd touched him last

night. How she'd whispered words of love in his
ear. The fervor in her words hadn't been a lie. Rachel did love him.

The image of Rachel's bruised face slashed
across his mind. The rage that had pumped so hot
and fast gave way to a bone-crushing sadness.
Only an animal would put that kind of a mark on
a woman.

His shoulders sagging, he sat on the edge of
the bed.

Small wonder she hadn't trusted him. He fisted
a handful of bedsheet in his hand as he pictured her
living with a man like that, the spirit and fire draining out of her day by day.

God help her, she'd had the courage to run.
She'd survived the shipwreck and had forged a
new life here in a village so foreign to her old life.
Even when the others hadn't wanted her, she'd
stayed. Long shadows cut across the stairway.

And he'd sent her away.

Memories of her haunted him. He remembered
the days he'd watched her hanging sheets on the
lines as the wind whipped her skirts around her ankles. The night she'd danced at the wedding reception, laughing as she moved expertly through the
dances. And most vivid, the look of surprised pleasure when she'd climaxed last night.

He couldn't imagine himself loving another woman as he did Rachel.

Save for the clock ticking in the hallway and the wind blowing outside, a deadly quite shrouded the house.

He pictured the rest of his life without Rachel—alone, manning the light, living among the villagers as they married and moved on with their lives.

An unbearable sadness settled on his shoulders.

Rachel had become a part of him—the half that made him whole.

Ben had to find her.

And prayed she would forgive him.

Rachel's heart slammed against her ribs. Peter! "How did you find me?"

He wrapped his long, smooth hands around her neck and pulled her back against his chest. His lips brushed her ear. "Forever and always."

"The ring. The captain."

He nipped her ear with his teeth. "He's a hearty sea captain, who knows how to survive. Though when I alert my men in Washington, he will find himself at the bottom of the Potomac River now."

"You're going to kill him."

"You know how I hate untidiness. Besides, he was a greedy sort. And I know his kind. He'd have been back for more money one day, threatening to expose your flight and embarrass me."

He spun her around and grabbed her hand. He smoothed his soft hand over hers. "Calluses? You've debased yourself in too many ways, my dear."

She snatched her hand back. "I've learned that I can work and take care of myself."

"You've grown too bold."

"I've found myself."

"You've grown a spine since we last saw each other. But don't worry, by the time I am done with you, you will be quite biddable."

"Never again."

As if she hadn't spoken, he pulled the ring from his pocket. He shoved the ring on her finger, tearing and scratching her flesh. He wrapped his hand around hers and squeezed hard. "Until death us do part, Rachel."

Her finger burned. The stones cut into her flesh. "I hate you. I'd rather die than return to Washington with you."

The lighthouse beacon flashed on the path.

Peter laughed. "Funny you should say that. I hadn't considered taking you back to Washington."

Cold fear shot through her body. "What have you got planned?"

An unholy pleasure gleamed in his stark blue

eyes. She could feel his arousal pressing against her. "You're nothing like the woman who left me. Coarse, unrefined, a tramp. And your beautiful hair." He ran his hand over the shorter tresses. Shivers snaked down her spine. "You shouldn't have cut it." He wrenched her arm behind her back, making her wince. "No, you aren't going back to Washington with me. I've got more creative ideas about what to do with you."

She forced herself to lift her chin. She'd never beg. "What are you going to do, Peter?"

"First, we are going to find a nice, quiet and very secluded spot. Then I'm going to teach you a lesson about disobedience." He glanced around the barren countryside. "I can see why you chose this place to hide. It's so wonderfully secluded. We shouldn't have any trouble finding privacy. Now, be a good girl and come along with me. I promise to make your death quick."

She jerked back, surprising him enough that she freed one hand. "I won't make this easy for you."

Anger warmed her blood. How dare he come back into her life and threaten her? In their marriage, she'd given in to his brutality. But no more. She'd die fighting.

Peter pulled a rope from his coat pocket. "I'd hoped you'd say that."

He yanked her forward with surprising strength. He tied the rope around her first wrist. The rope cut into her skin.

Survival instincts took over. If he got the rope around her wrists, she'd be helpless. And by daybreak she'd be dead.

Rachel raised her booted foot and drove her heel into his shin. The unexpected pain made him fumble with the rope. Peter cursed. He reached for her hair, but underestimated the length. She skirted forward out of his reach.

"Bitch!" he shouted. "You are going to pay for that very dearly."

She had no doubt death at his hands would be slow and painful. She stumbled forward and started to run. He snatched at her skirts. Fabric ripped. She screamed and yanked free.

The beacon flashed.

Rachel glanced up toward the lighthouse. Ben. She had to find him. She started to run down the path.

Peter growled his frustration and started after her. His feet pounded the dirt path.

She'd traveled the path hundreds of times in the past few weeks and she'd come to learn every root and every hole. Even with little moonlight she dodged the protruding roots and sandy holes.

Peter was faster, but he didn't know the path. He stripped, hitting the ground hard.

"Rachel," he screeched.

The pure evil in his voice rattled her. She stumbled but didn't fall. She kept running. Her side ached and her legs cramped, but she kept moving.

Rachel reached the base of the lighthouse and ran up the five steps to the open door. She didn't question why the door that Ben always kept closed was open. She ran inside and slammed the door shut. She fumbled with the bolt but her trembling hands couldn't budge it. Outside, she heard Peter running toward her, calling her name.

"Ben!" she shouted as she tried to move the latch.

No answer.

"Ben, please! Help me."

Silence.

Abandoning the door, she ran past the oil reserve tanks to the base of the winding staircase. She glanced up the spiral, praying Ben waited at the top. She screamed his name again. Where are you? She started to climb.

Ben had just reached the back porch of the cottage when he heard a man scream Rachel's name. In the moonlight he saw the shadowy fig-

ure reach the lighthouse door. The figure hesitated and looked back at Ben before he burst
through the door.

Rachel's muffled scream echoed from the tower
before the door slammed shut.

Panic exploded in his chest.

Ben ran to the lighthouse. He vaulted up the
brick steps of the base two at a time and reached
for the door. It was locked.

Rachel's head swam by the time she reached the
top of the lighthouse. Her side ached and sweat ran
down her back. She glanced down the spiral stair-
case and saw Peter. He'd found a lantern and lit it.
He'd climbed halfway up the stairs.

In that instant he stopped and glanced up at her.
Lantern light glowed off his pale features con-
torted with rage and excitement. He enjoyed this.
"You are trapped now.

"The lightkeeper isn't up there. I saw him running across the lawn. He looked quite worried." He
started to climb the stairs. This time he didn't
hurry. "Looks like it's just you and me, Rachel,"
he said.

Outside, she heard Ben pounding on the door,
shouting her name.

Tears welled in Rachel's eyes. She pressed the

heel of her hand into her eyes. *Don't panic. Don't panic.*

She glanced around the oval room that housed the oil tanks that powered the lenses. She needed a weapon. There was nothing except a heavy metal bucket Ben used to haul supplies up the stairs. She grabbed the bucket and ran toward the smaller staircase leading to the room that housed the tall lights. Sucking in a breath, she forced her muscles to work. She climbed the last ten steps to the light chamber.

The bright light flashed.

"Rachel!" Peter's voice sounded close. He'd reached the chamber below.

Taking her bucket, she went outside to the crow's nest. The wind blew hard. She glanced over the low railing and saw Ben below. He hammered the door with an anvil.

Rachel's hands were slick with sweat and she backed away from the door that led from the light chamber.

Peter's fine leather shoes echoed in the chamber. She took in a breath and forced herself to stop. Her heart pounded in her chest, mingling with the sound of Ben's hammer.

Peter moved closer. "Killing you is going to be a sweat pleasure."

From inside the lighthouse, a loud crash sounded as the door below banged open and slammed against the wall.

Ben.

Peter chuckled. "Seems your hero is almost here. You know what? I think I'm going to share the pleasure of your death with your lover. I'll make him watch as I bleed the life from your body. Then I'm going to kill him."

Anger gave Rachel courage. Peter was a monster. And he had to be stopped here and now before he hurt anyone she cared about. She lifted the bucket over her head.

Peter stepped out onto the crow's nest.

Rachel swung the bucket and hit him in the head as hard as she could. He stumbled toward the railing, clutching the bleeding side of his head. She ran toward him and pushed him.

His arms flayed as he tried to catch himself. His gaze locked briefly on hers. And then he fell two hundred feet to the ground below.

Ben heard a man's scream as he dashed up the last few steps to the crow's nest. He peered over the edge of the railing. Below lay the man he'd seen chasing Rachel. He lay on his back, his limbs and neck twisted. He was dead.

He found Rachel squatting, her back against the lighthouse. Her eyes were squeezed tight and her arms wrapped around her chest. Tears streaked her face.

He went to her and touched her shoulder. Her eyes flew open as she raised her fists. She started to strike out blindly. He absorbed her first blows before he captured her wrists. "Rachel, it's Ben."

She continued to struggle. "I won't die. I won't let you kill me."

Ben wrapped his arms around her and held her tight against his chest. "Rachel, it's Ben. Everything is going to be all right."

A shudder passed through her body. Her muscles relaxed. "Ben?"

"Yes, sweetheart, it's me."

"Where is Peter?" She strained against him. "I saw him fall."

He loosened his hold "He went over the side. He's dead. You don't want to look."

"Are you sure?"

"Yes."

She pulled away from him and staggered to her feet. "I need to see. I need to know that he is truly dead."

"Rachel don't."

She didn't hear him. "I have to go."

He followed her down the long twisting stair-case. He stayed right behind her, ready to catch her if she fell. But her steps were quick and deliberate as she hurried down the last steps, across the tiled floor and out the door.

He trailed behind her as she went around the side to Peter's body. She stared at it for several long minutes, as if she couldn't believe it. Then she yanked off her ring and tossed it on Peter's body.

Ben came behind her. He laid his hands on her shoulders. She flinched and pulled away. He felt so helpless. "It's over, Rachel. He is gone. You are free."

Rachel faced Ben. Her face looked so pale in the moonlight. "Free. I never believed I'd ever be free."

"Let me take you home," he said, holding out his hand to her.

She stood as inflexible as a statue. "I don't have a home," she said. "You told me to leave."

Her quietly spoken words hit him squarely in the chest. He wanted to hold her. But her body was so rigid he feared she'd break if he tried to touch her.

"I was upset," he said. "Add to that wounded pride and arrogance, and you've got a fool. I'm sorry."

"I needed you to love me and to understand."

"Rachel, you cannot leave like this. We need to

talk." He stabbed his fingers through his hair. "I was on my way to find you before *he* came."

She looked up at him. "Peter planned to kill you, too. I couldn't let that happen."

Her hair hung loosely around her face. Angry scratches marred her left hand. The marks sent a fresh wave of anger boiling inside him. He took her left hand in his and gently rubbed the mark left by the ring. "Dear Lord, I expected you to trust me when you had that monster after you. I am sorry. You have every right to be afraid, to be cautious."

Tears welled in her eyes. "I should have told you the truth." She wiped a tear from her face. "I wanted to so many times. But I feared you would look at me differently—that you wouldn't want me."

He took her in his arms and held her close. His body remained tense from the fight. "I've wanted you from the moment I woke up and saw you sleeping in my bed. Rachel, I love you. Nothing will ever change the way I feel about you."

She turned her face up to his. Her eyes looked expectant. "You still want me after all this? Peter hasn't tainted this place for you? Tainted me?"

"Never." He wiped a tear from her face. "He can't ruin anything unless we let him. He is the past. We are the future."

She laid her cheek against his chest. "The sheriff must be contacted. I killed him."

He could feel her heart hammering against his chest. "He will see that you acted in self-defense."

She pulled back and looked up at him. "There were no witnesses."

Ben touched her chin. "There's me and I'll wager if the sheriff spoke to the villagers, he'd find that they, too, saw everything—that you acted only to save your own life."

"I love you."

He hugged her fiercely, as if realizing he could have lost her tonight. "You are my life, Rachel. I love you."

Epilogue

Present Day

Marilyn Mitchell stood in front of the lighthouse. The sweeping winds of March cut across the sandy soil over the scattered patches of grass. The once-bright beacon was dark, the black and white stripe that had identified the lighthouse to the ships chipped and the brick base cracked.

The tower that had served this coastline for well over one hundred years was crumbling.

"Beyond me why you'd want to take on a project like this."

Marilyn turned toward the real estate agent, Frances Tucker, a gray-haired woman with dark eyes and red lips. "She deserves more than to tumble into ruins. She deserves to be saved."

"Gonna cost you a fortune."

Marilyn shoved her hands into her pockets. "I've already set up a foundation. We started fundraising over a year ago. Work will begin on the cottage next week."

"Why this lighthouse? There are others that people *want* saved.

"My mother was born in the cottage. She lived here until it closed." Weather and neglect had dulled the whitewashed cottage. The front steps had caved in and the roof had collapsed on the north side.

Mrs. Tucker shifted so that her back faced the cold wind. She pulled a cough drop out of her pocket and popped it into her mouth. "Mitchell. You said your name is Mitchell."

"That's right. My mother was Sara Mitchell. My grandfather and great-grandfather were keepers here until the station closed in 1948."

Mrs. Tucker stamped her feet to ward off the cold. "Mind if we get back in the car?"

"No, of course not." They started to walk back toward Marilyn's Suburban.

Mrs. Tucker rubbed her hands together as Marilyn pulled the keys from her purse. Silly to lock the car out here, but living in Washington had ingrained certain habits.

"I've heard tales about both men. Ben Mitchell was quite the hero."

Marilyn smiled. "He and my great-grandmother Rachel are credited with over a hundred rescues." She unlocked the car and they climbed in. Out of the wind, she warmed immediately.

Mrs. Tucker rubbed her gloved hands together. "Rachel Mitchell was the one who saved three fisherman when she was six months pregnant with her first child."

"Ben had been on the mainland that day. She was carrying my uncle. He was born a month early and still weighed eight pounds, according to the family bible."

Marilyn had grown up with stories of Rachel and Ben Mitchell. Ben had been awarded the Medal of Honor from the U.S. Coast Guard for his many rescues. Rachel Mitchell, featured in several books, had become a legend of sorts. She'd started the first school on the island, given birth and raised four children, and worked beside her beloved Ben for the fifty-seven years of their marriage.

"This lighthouse deserves to be saved."

Mrs. Tucker stared out the windshield at the lighthouse. "You've got a lot of work ahead of you."

This land has magic. It is the perfect place to start over. The words from Rachel's journal came to mind.

Marilyn started the car engine. "We Mitchells aren't afraid of hard work."

* * * * *

If you enjoyed what you just read,
then we've got an offer you can't resist!

Take 2 bestselling
love stories FREE!

Plus get a FREE surprise gift!

Clip this page and mail it to Harlequin Reader Service®

IN U.S.A.	IN CANADA
3010 Walden Ave.	P.O. Box 609
P.O. Box 1867	Fort Erie, Ontario
Buffalo, N.Y. 14240-1867	L2A 5X3

YES! Please send me 2 free Harlequin Historicals® novels and my free surprise gift. After receiving them, if I don't wish to receive anymore, I can return the shipping statement marked cancel. If I don't cancel, I will receive 6 brand-new novels every month, before they're available in stores! In the U.S.A., bill me at the bargain price of $4.69 plus 25¢ shipping and handling per book and applicable sales tax, if any*. In Canada, bill me at the bargain price of $5.24 plus 25¢ shipping and handling per book and applicable taxes**. That's the complete price and a savings of over 10% off the cover prices—what a great deal! I understand that accepting the 2 free books and gift places me under no obligation ever to buy any books. I can always return a shipment and cancel at any time. Even if I never buy another book from Harlequin, the 2 free books and gift are mine to keep forever.

246 HDN DZ7Q
349 HDN DZ7R

Name	(PLEASE PRINT)	
Address	Apt.#	
City	State/Prov.	Zip/Postal Code

Not valid to current Harlequin Historicals® subscribers.

Want to try two free books from another series?
Call 1-800-873-8635 or visit www.morefreebooks.com.

* Terms and prices subject to change without notice. Sales tax applicable in N.Y.
** Canadian residents will be charged applicable provincial taxes and GST.
   All orders subject to approval. Offer limited to one per household.
   ® are registered trademarks owned and used by the trademark owner and or its licensee.

HIST04R   ©2004 Harlequin Enterprises Limited